ESCAPE FROM
MERCY
HALL

Also by
Garth Edwards

The Adventures of Titch & Mitch

THE THORN GATE TRILOGY

BOOK ONE

ESCAPE FROM MERCY HALL

by
Garth Edwards

with illustrations by
Max Stasyuk

Published in Great Britain by
Inside Pocket Publishing Limited

First published in Great Britain 2011
Text copyright © Garth Edwards 2011

The right of Garth Edwards to be identified as
the author of this work has been asserted
by him in accordance with the
Copyright, Designs and Patents Act 1988

Illustrations copyright © Inside Pocket Publishing Limited 2011

A CIP catalogue record for this book is available from
the British Library

ISBN 978 0956 71224 0

Inside Pocket Publishing Limited Reg. No. 06580097

Printed and bound in Great Britain by
CPI Bookmarque Ltd, Croydon

www.insidepocket.co.uk

CONTENTS

PROLOGUE

The boy was lost.

He had been told to follow the path and keep going along the side of the hedge until he came to a bench. There he was to sit and wait for the coach.

The great thorn hedge stretched out of sight as he followed the path until his legs felt tired, but he could find no bench.

It was beginning to grow dark and cold.

He scratched his head and thought. Had he turned the wrong way? Had he already passed the bench?

Beginning to feel hungry, he wondered if perhaps he shouldn't turn around and head back. Perhaps it would be better to start this journey in the morning.

Then he heard a crackling sound. He turned to see a strange light glowing from within the hedge; a curious, powerful light that got brighter and more intense as the crackling noise got louder and louder.

And then the hedge opened...

I

ESCAPE IN THE DARK

Sam lay on his bed and strained his ears for any sound. A sudden scuffing noise of feet on gravel made him sit up. Throwing the bedclothes to one side, he darted to the window. In the moonlight he saw a slight figure running down the drive, a blanket draped over its shoulders.

'George,' he hissed as loud as he dared. 'Milly is running away.'

The boy who shared his room was George Price, a small but agile boy, with a sharp mind and keen instinct. He rose quickly and joined Sam at the window.

Earlier that night, Milly had been sent to her room in tears by the head of the orphanage, so it came as no surprise to either of them seeing her trying to make an escape.

'She's talked about running away for a long time,' said George.

'But matron locked the door to Milly's room,' said Sam. 'How did she get out?'

George frowned. 'I don't know, but she's bound to be caught if we don't help her.'

There was no time for further discussion. As they quickly dressed, Sam tried to think of a way out of the building. He had just decided to break a window on the ground floor when George joined him at the door.

'The fire escape is the only door not locked,' said George, as if he could read Sam's thoughts. 'I'm certain Milly turned off the main drive. She must have taken the path through the woods towards the hedge.'

Pulling their jackets tight to protect themselves from the cold, damp night, the two boys raced after their fleeing friend. Stumbling along the dark, wooded path, they reached the giant thorn hedge that bordered the orphanage and its grounds. It was a huge hedge, at least twice their height, and neither boy could remember ever having seen anything on the other side of it. The thorn hedge was the very edge of their world, a dark forbidding edge, full of danger and uncertainty.

They ran alongside the hedge until, in the light of a full moon, they caught a glimpse of Milly some way ahead of them.

'Milly,' roared George. 'Come back!'

The shadowy figure in the distance stopped and turned. Immediately the boys slowed their mad sprint down to a jog. Milly had stopped at a place where the hedge curved around a large elm tree before continuing its line along the perimeter. As they approached, she raised a hand to show she recognised them. At the same time, a light appeared from inside the hedge and illuminated her in an eery glow. The boys stopped in surprise. Suddenly there was a loud noise like the crackling of a million breaking twigs. Milly turned to see the branches within the dense hedge transform from a tangled mass into a curtain of smooth, straightened sticks that stretched to the very top.

The two boys stood rooted to the spot and stared in amazement as the light grew brighter and the gap between the sticks widened. Sam snapped out of his trance.

'Milly,' he shouted. 'Get away from the hedge!'

Before she could move, three tall, hooded figures, dressed in long orange robes, stepped out from the light and surrounded her. They paused momentarily, towering over Milly like sentinels, then grabbed hold of her arms and dragged her towards the opening. Milly screamed long and loud.

Without a thought for their own safety, the two boys charged after them. The mysterious light on the other side illuminated the struggling figure of Milly, being bundled away.

'Stop!' screeched Sam in a rage. 'Leave her alone!'

'Aaaaah,' was all George could say as he launched himself to the rescue.

For a moment there was chaos.

The abductors dropped Milly to defend themselves. Sam ran headfirst into what seemed like a gatepost, causing it to snap. George crashed into Sam. The would-be kidnappers recovered themselves first. The light began to sway and move off. Then, with a sudden loud hissing noise, it shot forward and moved rapidly away from them, disappearing into the darkness.

'Are you all right?' asked Sam, as he helped Milly to her feet.

'Yes, I think so. But I was so frightened,' she said. The slimly built girl had a pretty, freckled face and short plaits. At ten years old, she was a year younger than the boys and, despite her slender frame, could be tough and resolute. Her biggest problem was the way she liked to act on impulse; this had landed her in trouble from the day she arrived at the orphanage and was probably the reason why Sam liked her so much.

'Are you sure you're all right?' asked George. He was concerned, and putting his hands on her shoulders, looked her closely in the eye.

She nodded back at him and gave a tired smile. 'I'm fine. I'm sorry to have caused you all this trouble. I was only running away.'

A loud crackling sound stopped all their talk.

'Quick,' called out George. 'The hedge is closing. We'd better get back.'

Before they could move, the crackling noise grew louder and, as they watched, the long, slim poles rapidly bent in all directions. Branches twisted and the thorns stretched out again. In just a few moments the crackling stopped and the hedge was back to normal; huge, dense and totally impenetrable.

'What do we do now?' asked Sam.

'We could just walk along the hedge until we find a way through, I suppose,' suggested George.

'Nobody has ever been through the thorn hedge before,' said Milly. 'We all know that.'

'Maybe we should wait until morning. Perhaps we can make the hedge open up again,' suggested

George. 'Somebody or something caused it to open, so we know there is a way through, somehow.'

Sam considered the idea, but could not help feeling less positive than his friend about their chances. He liked his roommate a lot; George was always helpful and never lost his temper. He was older than Sam by just a month, and as he excelled in all the lessons at the orphanage, he was a great help to Sam, who usually took his advice. Sam himself was more keen on sports than on schoolwork, and certainly didn't like to wait. However, considering that George was probably right, he reluctantly agreed.

'I suppose we'd better wait here,' he said, slumping to the ground.

Milly took the blanket from her shoulders and laid it on the cool grass.

'It's quite a warm night, isn't it?' she observed, looking up at the twinkling stars above. 'I expected it to be cold.'

'That's some relief,' said George, as the boys joined her on the blanket. 'At least we won't freeze to death...'

There was a lot of talk and little sleep before morning arrived. All three of them were united in their hatred of the Mercy Hall Home for Orphans, and their desire to be free from its clutches.

The building itself was a large, rambling old house with poor heating, draughty windows and just a single gas light in each room. It would have been pulled down except that the government had recently decreed, in the name of the Queen herself, that orphaned children should be taken off the streets and educated by the parish or a suitable charity. So a charity had taken over the building and undertaken to provide a home and an education for the poor foundlings of the city in an environment of love and affection, except that the education was poor and the love and affection non-existent.

The headmaster of the orphanage was a large, fearsome man by the name of Jethro Barking. He was well over six feet tall, wore dark, pin-striped suits with frayed cuffs and greasy lapels and walked with a limp on his left side. On account of this limp, he was never seen without his cane, which he would also use to beat the children on the slightest pretext. He was a greedy man, whose main pleasure in life seemed to be eating. His meals were taken in a private room that he shared with Maude Jones, the matron and secretary of the home, and his main ally in the apparent campaign against the children's well-being.

Maude Jones was a gaunt woman with cold, steely eyes and thin, pale lips. The only person she ever smiled at was the headmaster, especially when supervising the delivery of his meals. The kitchen staff prepared the food for him and, under Maude's watchful gaze, carried it through the main dining room, past the twenty four orphans waiting for their meal, and into the private rooms of Mr Barking.

The delicious smell of roast meats, freshly baked pies, trifles and exotic fruits taunted the children every day. When the door to the private rooms closed the orphans would line up, bowls in hand, to receive a ladle of porridge for breakfast, cold mashed potatoes and stew for lunch, and bread with a thin film of dripping for tea. The diet was never varied, except at Christmas, when a cold slice of chicken was added to the porridge.

Old Barking Mad, or OBM, as the orphans called him, hated children. This was well known because he told them so in a strident voice every day at morning assembly. He would stride up and down the dining hall, his pin-striped suit still flecked with the remnants of yesterday's dinner, swishing his beloved cane from left to right with each step.

'Good for nothing, that's what you lot are!' he would cry, his face red as beetroot. 'You're lucky I don't throw you all out!'

The children, sitting quiet and still on their cold, hard benches, felt much the same way about Barking, though none ever dared say it out loud.

Stuck on the far side of a hedge, in a place they had never seen before, Sam, George and Milly discussed the earlier incident that had upset her so much and started her on this flight for freedom.

It had involved the untimely demise of Scruffy, a small dog she'd kept hidden in the home. Pets of course were not allowed, but Milly's older brother

Tom had found the poor animal in a ditch some months ago and brought him back, soaking wet and covered in mud. He was a wire-haired terrier, mostly white in colour, with patches of black over his head and shoulders. Tom had sneaked round to the back of the orphanage and smuggled him into the building. There was a storeroom at the side of the back door, which was locked but, as Tom knew, the key was always kept in a jar on the window ledge. He decided that the room was the ideal place to help restore the poor creature back to health.

The fact that the dog never barked and always hid away if he saw an adult coming meant that he survived and prospered in his snug home. The children, each sworn to secrecy by Tom, looked after him and fed him with whatever scraps they could smuggle from the kitchens. It was Milly who'd named him Scruffy.

Not long afterwards, the headmaster informed Tom that a position had been found for him as an apprentice printer to a firm in London. As he had just reached his fourteenth birthday it was time for him to leave the home and make his way in the world. Tom and Milly were very upset at being parted, but when Tom pointed out that he would send for her as soon as he could, Milly realised that her time at the orphanage would soon come to an end and she had cheered up enormously.

Scruffy became her responsibility and, for the following weeks and months she cared for him as best she could, taking him out for short walks in the evenings and early mornings, and giving him all the spare scraps she could muster.

But as the months passed by, and no letter of any sort came for Milly, she began to grow disheartened. She could not understand why Tom did not write. Eventually, she confided in Sam that one day soon she would run away to London and go and find her brother herself. If there was no one to care for the dog, she would take him with her. In her sadness, she grew careless.

That evening, as she had gone to take Scruffy some food, a pair of cold, hard eyes was watching. Maude Jones liked animals even less than OBM liked children.

Sam and George witnessed the scene that followed. Most of the children were just sitting down to eat when the matron dragged Milly and Scruffy through the dining hall. The headmaster, still in his private room, lumbered out, wiping gravy from his chin, when Maude Jones screamed for him to come and see what she had found.

The face of Jethro Barking pulsed with rage when he saw the dog. His cheeks grew redder on discovering the creature had been living in the storeroom for such a long time. The cane was raised high in the air and brought whistling down in a vicious blow that struck Milly across the shoulders. She screamed and tried to escape, but Maude gripped her arm with bony, vice-like fingers. Twice more the cane landed across Milly's back. Only when all the children in the room cried out in protest and anger did the headmaster stop. Spitting phlegm and dripping sweat, Old Barking Mad turned on them. 'You will all pay dearly for this outrage, mark my words,' he snarled.

Ordering Maude to lock Milly in her room, he grabbed Scruffy by the neck and strode out of the hall.

All the children were ordered to bed immediately without even being fed. But locking Milly's door was never going to stop her from running away. Already used to sneaking out, she could easily open the bedroom window and knew how to climb down to the ground without disturbing a soul.

The children's conversation had come full circle, and they found themselves asking the same questions of each other: what had happened at the hedge? Who were the strange people in orange robes who had tried to drag Milly away? How could a hedge open and close by itself?

With no clear answers to guide them, soon all three of them lapsed into silence.

'Well,' said Sam finally. 'I daresay we'll find out a little bit more tomorrow, hey?' Then he curled himself up and settled down to get some sleep. Milly and George huddled together and eventually they too drifted into a restless sleep on the thin blanket.

2

INTO A STRANGE LAND

The sun announced the start of a new day, like a light being switched on. After walking up and down the hedge for a while, Milly, Sam and George could find no way through, nor any way to make the branches straighten out.

Sam found the remains of the gatepost he had broken when he burst through the hedge. 'This is what stopped us last night,' he said, picking it up and tossing it aside.

Milly produced a few scraps of bread, which they shared gratefully. The excitement of the encounter in the thorn hedge had worn off. George turned to his two friends with a look of deep concern. 'There's something not quite right here,' he said, looking around.

'What do you mean?' asked Sam.

'There must be houses and people somewhere nearby,' said George. 'Look at the grass.'

'What's wrong with the grass?' asked Sam, puzzled.

George gestured around. 'There's nothing wrong with it. It's perfect,' he said. 'We are walking on a neat, well kept lawn, but there are no houses anywhere in sight. We think nobody lives behind the thorn hedge because there is no way to get through it. There's no gate, no road and no path. So why is the grass so short? Who cuts the grass?'

Sam and Milly looked around a little more. The hedge loomed above them, stretching away in both directions. It seemed to meet up with a cliff on one side and drop down into a valley on the other.

'He's right,' said Milly at last. 'Everything is so... tidy.'

'I say we head for those trees over there,' said Sam, pointing at a small clump of woodland down in the valley. 'We may find something there.'

The others agreed and off they set, but before they had gone more than a few yards George stopped and turned back towards the hedge.

'In case we need to find this spot again,' he said thoughtfully, 'there ought to be something we can recognise.' Taking a white handkerchief from his pocket, he walked back to the hedge and, reaching up as high as he could, he tied it to a branch that jutted out slightly from the rest.

'There. That should do it.'

Milly and Sam agreed and, once again, the three of them set off. The morning sun warmed their bones and cheered them slightly; for a moment they even forget that they were actually quite hungry.

After walking for an hour or so they were worn out; the wood had been further away than they had expected, and now they found themselves walking up towards the brow of another hill. They thought to rest for a while but decided to keep going, hoping to find signs of life on the other side. As they reached the top of the hill, a bell started to tinkle somewhere to their left, making them jump. Turning, they spotted what looked like a roman chariot racing towards them. As it got closer they saw it had a single driver and was pulled by a small pony. It drove straight at them with the driver standing up to his full height, which wasn't very high at all, and clanging his tiny bell. Finally it pulled up in front of Milly and came to a shuddering halt.

Glowering at them with his small eyes, the driver snorted brusquely, and so did the horse.

'Would that strange female creature kindly remove herself from my road,' he said, snorting once again then sniffing sharply. The look of the man, for he was clearly fully grown, was altogether most angular, with a sharp nose, thin lips and a firm and very pointed beard covering what was sure to be a very sharp chin. His arms and legs, though obviously quite strong, seemed far too long for his skinny body. He was wearing a tight, yellow tunic, laced down the front, and matching yellow shorts that exposed very bony knees.

'Go around her,' suggested George, really trying to be helpful. 'There is no road.'

The little man looked at him with undisguised contempt and, raising a long, bony finger, pointed the way ahead.

'My road, young sir, cannot be moved.'

Turning to see where he was pointing, the children saw a long line of tiny, flashing lights which were half hidden by the grass and stretched out in a straight line as far as the eye could see.

'My road ahead,' confirmed the man.

Following the lights back to where they stood, the children noticed something odd about the chariot. It was indeed shaped like a Roman one, but it had no wheels, nor any other means of support. Instead, it floated clear above the ground to a height of about one foot.

They all spoke at once.

'Where are your wheels?' asked Sam pointing at the space where the wheels should have been. 'How do you stay suspended off the ground?'

'Where did the lights come from?' asked Milly, as she obligingly stepped aside. 'I don't recall seeing them before. Are they candles?'

'Who are you? Where have you come from?' asked George.

'My name is Klaxon. I have come from my home and now I need to be on my way,' said the man, gathering his reigns. 'You have delayed me long enough.' With that, he gave a small flick of the wrist and called out, 'Hey up, Klaxonhorse. Let's be off!'

The pony snorted and jerked its head up and down. Before it could move however, Sam stepped in front of it, taking the place vacated by Milly, and held up both hands.

'I am very sorry, Mr Klaxon,' he said firmly. 'But we need some information.'

'For a start,' added George, 'what do you know about the thorn hedge back there?' He pointed in the direction they had come. 'Who planted it?'

'The hedge has always been there,' said Klaxon in irritation. 'It's to protect the people from the land of giants.'

Three young faces looked suddenly very shocked. Klaxon warmed to his theme.

'Behind that hedge lies a cold, dark land of rain and snow, where cruel giants kill and eat innocent animals. They live on the edge of the world and, when there are too many giants, they push all the old giants over the edge into a pit of fire!' He shivered at the very thought. 'I wouldn't go there if I were you.'

They were all taken aback by this answer, but George persisted with questions.

'Why couldn't we see the road earlier?' he asked. 'And why hasn't your chariot got any wheels?'

'Wheels?' shot back the increasingly irritated Klaxon. 'I don't need wheels! Never have used wheels, not on a magneto road, and all the roads that go anywhere around here are magneto roads.'

George looked under the chariot. A metal plate hummed with energy. All the carts and coaches George had ever seen had wheels and were pulled by large horses. He really couldn't believe his eyes.

'It's the strangest thing I've ever seen,' he muttered. But stranger still was yet to come, for another voice spoke and startled them completely.

'Would you please get out of the way! I need

some food and a rest and have no wish to be kept waiting any longer!'

For a pony to speak is one thing. For a pony to speak and sound like a normal human being is quite another.

Sam stepped forward and put his head a few centimetres from the pony's face. 'You can speak!' he said in astonishment.

'Of course I speak!' replied the animal gruffly. 'How could a proper creature live anywhere without speaking? How could Klaxon tell me where to go? How would he know when I'm hungry or want a rest? Would he buy a horse like me if I couldn't speak?'

'I...' Sam tried to reply, but the words simply wouldn't come.

'You're a bit small for a horse,' said George. 'We thought you were a pony.'

'I assure you I am a horse,' replied the animal testily.

'Do all animals here speak?' asked Milly, who also found it hard to accept that a horse could talk. 'Even things like worms and spiders?'

Klaxon sighed in exasperation. 'He meant proper creatures like you and me, not creepy-crawlies or Muttons or flying Tick-Tocks.'

'Flying Tick-Tocks?' repeated George, trying to imagine a clock with wings.

Klaxon eyed them with suspicion. 'You aren't young giants from over the hedge are you?' he asked with an expression of alarm spreading over his face.

'Because if you are, I have to alert the Robes and they'll make sure you all get pegged out.'

Ignoring him, George pointed in the direction of the hedge and changed the subject with another question. 'Why are there clouds on the other side of the hedge, but no clouds on this side? And why is it warm and sunny here, yet on the other side it's cold?'

'I don't know, it's always warm and sunny here,' replied Klaxon, his voice beginning to quake a little. 'You are new to Littlewich, aren't you?'

'Little what?' asked Sam, never having heard the name before.

'Littlewich!' snarled the horse.

'Yes, and we are a bit lost,' admitted George.

Sam decided to be direct and straightforward. 'We are not young giants, but we came through the hedge this morning when all the branches straightened up. We want to go back again,' he added sharply. It was getting near lunchtime and he always got a little tetchy when hungry.

'My friend wants to know how can we get back through the hedge? Is there a proper path we can use?' Milly spoke politely, putting on her most agreeable voice.

'Nobody can get through the hedge,' replied Klaxon. Then he thought for a moment and added, 'Unless of course the Robes can.'

'Who are the Robes?' asked George.

'You really should avoid the Robes,' Klaxon's voice softened and he began to sound almost friendly. But, before he could elaborate, the horse lost patience with his lack of progress and, lowering his head, stepped forward and butted Sam firmly in the chest.

'Out of my way,' he snorted. 'I'm hungry and we have to get to Littlewich without delay.'

Sam fell to the ground and rolled out of the way as the tiny horse trotted forward and gathered speed. Klaxon smiled graciously at the three friends as the chariot glided past them.

'Who cuts the grass?' shouted George after them.

Klaxon looked over his shoulder at them. 'The Muttons come out and eat the grass every night,' he shouted back. 'They'll be delighted to see you. They eat everything they find.' He laughed so loudly they could still hear the cackling as the chariot disappeared into the distance.

'This is really quite bizarre,' said Sam, scratching his head and looking bewildered. 'What is this place?

We come through a hedge and its like walking into a different world.'

'Maybe it is a different world,' added Milly. 'But how on earth do we get back?'

'Do we want to go back?' asked George. 'We have no family to worry about us, no proper home to go to. I daresay we will go back eventually, but right now these new things are a bit exciting, don't you think? I vote we explore a bit more.'

'I'm hungry!' added Sam. 'I vote we go to this Littlewich and get some food, then we can decide what to do. The people who live there can't all be as unfriendly as Klaxon, or his silly animal.' Sam scuffed a foot along the grass as he spoke. 'Surely that was a trick with the horse, wasn't it?'

The others shrugged.

'The horse spoke,' said George. 'You heard it.'

Sam nodded. 'I think we have to see more of this place as well. What did he call it? Littlewich?'

'I'm not so sure,' said Milly, pulling the blanket tight around her shoulders and shivering despite the warmth of the sun. 'That last comment from Klaxon about Muttons eating everything they find has made me nervous. What is a mutton anyway?'

'Probably nonsense,' said George reassuringly. 'But let's get some food at least, or poor Sam here will starve.'

'All right,' she said, after a little thought. 'But at the first sign of trouble, we run. Agreed?'

'Agreed!' said the two boys firmly, neither of them having any idea where they might run too.

3

THE WAY TO LITTLEWICH

The twinkling lights in the grass were only visible if they kept walking towards them. If they strayed off the hidden road the lights disappeared and it was easy to get lost. An hour later they trudged over a ridge and saw the town of Littlewich in the distance. Sunshine reflected off rows of red roofs and little strings of smoke floated skywards in straight lines. A river ran past the town and under a narrow bridge where the road crossed before entering among the tightly clustered houses.

'Water,' cried George, pointing at the river. 'At least we can have a drink soon. Come on, let's hurry! We must get there before the shops close for the day.'

As the town loomed nearer they noticed a dog standing to one side of the magneto road and staring at them. From a distance it looked like a grey wolf, but as they got closer they saw it had big, floppy ears and quite a flat nose. It hung its head and sad brown eyes watched them approach.

Milly thought it looked quite miserable and went to stroke it.

'Careful, Milly,' called out George. 'It may bite.'

'Nonsense,' said Milly cheerfully, and stretching

out her hand she added, 'You're not going to bite me, are you old chap?'

'Of course I'm not,' said the dog, in a distinct and precise voice that startled all of them. 'Do you think me some sort of villain?'

Having convinced themselves that Klaxon's talking horse had been a trick, and the skinny little man himself a master ventriloquist, Milly jumped back quite startled.

'You can talk!' she exclaimed, somewhat louder than necessary.

The dog jerked its ears back and cocked its head to look at her quizzically. 'And I can hear well enough without you needing to shout,' it said, with a gruff shake of its head. His collar appeared to be giving him some discomfort.

The boys joined Milly and crowded round the dog all talking at once while they petted and stroked it.

'It is very nice of you to show such affection after so short an acquaintance,' said the dog. 'But we do have a problem.'

'What sort of problem?' asked George.

'If you look closely, you can see there is a collar around my neck which is attached to a chain, which itself is attached to a stake in the ground. You will also notice that I have been scrabbling desperately in an attempt to get the stake out of the ground, so that I no longer have to stand here and get eaten. Alas, all my efforts have been in vain. When I saw you approaching, I hoped that you might be kind enough to help me.'

'Indeed we will!' cried Milly without a second's thought, and immediately tried to remove the collar from around the dog's neck. Unfortunately, it was tied tightly together with stiff wire and her fingers couldn't undo it. Sam tried as well but couldn't loosen it either, so he grabbed the stake and tried to heave it out of the ground. Despite heaving it to and fro with all his might, it would not move at all.

'Here, let me help,' said George, and together they both tried to pull it out, but still it would not budge. Milly joined in and they yanked and pushed and pulled till they were all quite exhausted, but all to no avail; the stake remained firmly embedded in the ground.

The dog stood and watched them sadly, already knowing their actions to be futile.

After much pushing and shoving, they had to admit defeat and sat down on the grass for a rest.

'Perhaps we can get help from the town?' suggested Sam.

'It was the people in the town that put me here,' said the dog, with growing desperation in its voice. 'And besides, there is no time. If you can't get the stake out quickly, you had better run into Littlewich and save yourselves. Nobody there will help a slave dog, especially one as wicked as me.'

Milly kneeled beside the dog. 'You poor thing,' she said, stroking the dog's back. 'But don't worry, we are not going to leave you staked out here all night.'

'You're a very kind girl. May I enquire as to your name?'

Milly introduced herself and the two boys and began to tell him the story of how they came to be there, but before she got very far, the dog raised a paw to silence her.

'My name is Drago, and I would love to hear your whole story, fascinating as it sounds. Alas, there is no more time.' He let his head fall to his chest.

'Why did you say we need to run to save ourselves?' asked George, who suddenly felt very nervous.

Looking up again, Drago stared intently ahead. 'Because the Muttons are out a bit early today,' he said, in a voice flat and resigned.

Turning round they saw a number of white, woolly sheep grazing the grass and moving slowly towards them.

'They're just a bunch of sheep,' said Sam. 'They can't hurt anybody.'

'Your bravery astounds me,' said Drago. 'But I suspect you haven't seen the Muttons before.'

'Well no, but we have lots like them where we come from.' He looked again, suddenly becoming a little uncertain about the approaching animals. There was something about them that didn't quite fit with his idea of sheep in general.

'I'm afraid you must run away and leave me here,' said Drago sadly. 'Once we are surrounded there is no escape.'

The two boys stood up and looked at each other

nervously. Milly tugged at their sleeves. 'Come on,' she said urgently. 'George, think of something.'

Looking at her anxious face, George stroked his chin and furrowed his brow. 'I know, we'll try the leverage principal,' he said. 'We need to apply all our combined strength to pull the stake upwards. The chain is long enough, but we can't all pull up together. As Sam is the tallest, let's put the chain over his shoulder and the rest of us, including Drago, pull on the chain and try to pull him over. If he doesn't let go and we manage to drag him over, the stake should come out of the ground.'

Sam took a firm grip of the chain, slipped it over his shoulder and bent his knees. Behind him and a little way back, George did the same. Then, behind him, Milly took her tightest grip. At the end of the line, Drago braced himself to pull for his life.

'One, two, three... Heave!' called out George.

Nothing happened.

'Again,' shouted George.

As they heaved a second time, they heard a low growl coming from Drago that grew louder and louder as he pulled on the chain. With a sudden tearing noise the stake ripped out of the soil. Sam fell over backwards and George and Milly plumped down hard on the grass. Scrambling to their feet, they were so delighted with the success of their efforts, they cheered loudly.

But, when they turned round to face Drago, two things startled them.

Firstly, the Muttons were everywhere. At close

33

quarters the woolly sheep were totally different to what they expected. Their faces had razor sharp, triangular teeth set into a wide, thin mouth that turned up towards cruel, narrow eyes, giving the creature a permanently fixed smirk. It was not the face of a sheep at all, but the face of a predator! All the Muttons were staring at them now, and the nearest one licked its thin, slavering lips.

Secondly, the dog Drago had doubled in size. His chest had expanded and muscles rippled down his back and legs. The noise that came from his throat was a rumbling, angry growl and, while they watched, his lips drew back to expose huge, glistening fangs. Burning red eyes glared hard at the Muttons and he moved towards them on firm, powerful legs.

The three friends drew together, realising they were in enormous danger.

The Muttons were so close now that the children could smell their rank breath and see the snarl on their lips. Suddenly, Drago charged at the nearest Mutton and, with a dart of his head, fixed his teeth into its woolly neck. With a vicious shake the angry dog threw the wounded creature to one side and immediately swung round to attack the next Mutton.

At the same time the other Muttons rushed to attack the dog. As they did so, a gap opened up within the pack of fighting animals and the three children rushed through it to escape the mêlée. In leaps and bounds they reached open grass and carried on running as fast as they could. When they were sure there was no pursuit, they stopped to look back.

Drago had broken away from the fight and was limping towards them while the Muttons stayed together, huddled in a bunch. As the dog got further away, one by one they resumed munching the grass as if nothing had happened. George, Milly and Sam waited anxiously as Drago approached. He appeared to grow smaller with each step.

'Now you know who cuts the grass,' murmured Sam to George.

'The Muttons only move slowly,' said Drago, as he reached them, now back to his normal size, though short of breath. 'We'll be safe when we get to the road into town. Muttons never leave the grasslands.'

'You're hurt,' said Milly, spotting the red flecks of blood on Drago's back leg.

'It's just a bite,' said Drago, looking down. 'One of them got lucky. It's of no consequence.'

'What happened to you?' asked Sam. 'One minute you were a normal sized dog then, all of a sudden, you're twice the size, and now you're back to normal again.'

'It's a long story,' said Drago in a sad voice. Then looking behind at the Muttons, he added, 'Perhaps we should get off the grass and I'll tell you on the way.'

The light was beginning to fade as the children gathered round Drago and walked the rest of the way into town. George carried the stake and the chain, which was still attached to Drago's collar, so that it looked as though the dog was on a lead.

'I was a normal contented slave dog working for a Minling family way up north of here, when I was taken by the Robes. They needed me to guard a cargo they were taking back to Dome City. That's where they live, you know.'

'We didn't know actually,' chipped in Sam.

'We got on a boat in Littlewich and floated along

the river and into the mountain tunnel. When we came to the Rainbow Cave, we drifted through on the boat.'

'What's the Rainbow Cave?' interrupted Milly.

'I thought every creature in the land knew about the Rainbow Cave,' said Drago. 'You really are strange people! Where did you say you came from?'

'We'll tell you later,' said Milly. 'Please, what is the Rainbow Cave?'

'It's a big cave on the way to Dome City. Inside there is a great lake. Above this lake, high in the vaults of the cave, lights of many colours flicker and glow continuously. It is said that any creature who passes through this cave and sees the lights can... change.'

'How do you mean... change?'

'Creatures change, that is all. One never knows how they will change, sometimes nothing changes, but usually something happens. A creature can grow bigger or smaller, or cleverer, or suddenly see a very long way, or be enormously strong or very weak, or see in the dark. I don't know, there are many changes possible, and some of them may not be so beneficial.'

The dog lapsed into silence for a while.

'Did you change?' asked George, anxious for him to continue his story.

Drago shrugged.

'I saw the lights. They were beautiful, like nothing I'd ever seen before. But I felt nothing. No change came over me then. When I got back from my journey, I was simply a spare slave dog without an owner. The Robes didn't know what to do with me; nobody in the town wanted a stray slave dog. Then one of them kicked me, and I got angry... so they decided to peg me out and feed me to the Muttons.'

'That's terrible,' said Milly, shaking her head.

'That was the thanks I got. And then you came along.'

Drago stopped and turned to them, his eyes suddenly burning with excitement.

'You see, I thought I hadn't been changed by the Rainbow Cave at all, but I had, and it was when I got angry that I found out what it was: I get bigger and stronger and very fierce when threatened. And when the threat has gone, I return to normal. Quite a useful skill to have, don't you think?'

'That is fantastic,' said Sam, fired up by the very thought of changing into someone stronger.

'Unless you're a Robe... They don't like animals to change.'

'I find it all rather hard to believe,' added George, a little more doubtful of the whole idea. 'Where did you say this Rainbow Cave was?'

'Up river, beyond the town. Only the Robes can go through it safely. No Minlings ever go through it. They are too frightened.'

'Why?' asked Milly.

'Because they don't want to get changed, of course. Minlings don't like changes.'

'They let you go through'

'I'm a slave dog, which is different.'

'How?' asked George.

'I'm expendable. They can use me, then throw me away.'

'We won't throw you away,' promised Milly, giving the dog a hug.

The little group had reached the bridge that crossed the river and led into town. Conversation stopped while they all looked around and planned their next move.

4

THE ANGRY WAITER

The road leading into Littlewich was made of neatly compacted white stones polished and perfectly flat, making it very smooth and comfortable to walk on. In the centre of the road, the row of lights shone with a gently pulsing glow. The road was lined with small, neat houses, each with a window on either side of a brightly painted front door and two more above for the upstairs rooms. Each house was shaped like a large loaf of bread with a red roof and white walls. Some of the houses were shops, with neat signs above the door, such as Butcher, Baker, Candlestick Maker and so on. Otherwise there was nothing to distinguish them from domestic dwellings.

A few people, each of them similar in looks to Klaxon, wandered around from house to house going about their business. Their skinny bodies and long, thin arms and legs looked quite odd in the tight, brightly coloured tunics and narrow trousers they all wore. None of them were any bigger than the children, and quite a few were a fair bit smaller. Each carried a wicker basket into which they would stuff their purchases.

Some carts and carriages pulled by small horses

busied themselves down the centre of the street. Some of these carts had wheels with soft rubber tyres, which squeaked on the smooth stone surface as they moved slowly along. Others floated above the ground, just like Klaxon's had done.

A smaller cart containing three skinny children and being pulled by a dog passed by the visitors. The occupants could be heard having a disjointed conversation.

'Turn right, Smidgeons, I'm next,' said one of them leaning forward and tweaking the dog's tail.

'No, stop here Smidgeons, I want to buy some sweets,' said another.

'Keep going Smidgeons!' barked a third. 'I'm the eldest and you do as I say.' The young Minlings in the cart all stopped talking as they passed the friends and kept their eyes fixed on them until Smidgeons and the cart abruptly turned off the road and disappeared down a narrow lane between two houses.

'Drago, you've been here before. Where can we buy some food?' asked Sam, clutching his stomach in an effort to keep the hunger pangs away.

'And is there a hotel or lodging house in the town?' asked George, ever the more practical of the two. 'We're going to need somewhere to stay the night.'

'Follow me,' replied the dog. 'I know of an eating establishment not far away.'

Everything was so different to what they expected that they began to feel a little uneasy. It was amazing to hear horses talking to their drivers as carts and little coaches passed by. The place seemed like a medieval village of little people, stuck in a time warp.

They were just getting used to seeing it that way, when another skinny man walked towards them, effortlessly pushing a strange humming machine that sucked dirt and dust from the street. It also had two spinning mops that left behind a trail smoother and shinier than any road they had ever seen. They stared at this machine with eyes so wide that the little man pushing it grew quite panicky and pushed it away with increased speed.

Drago turned a corner and they arrived at what appeared to be the centre of the town. In the middle of a square there was a statue of a person dressed in a long robe standing on a pedestal. In one hand it clutched a sheaf of papers, the other was held outstretched, pointing far off into the distance. Around the square more of the Littlewich people were going about their business. A large building with a big open door indicated a town hall or something similar.

Just off the square Drago stopped at a small shop with a sign in the window which read, 'MEALS ALL DAY'. It was just what they needed. Without pausing, the three friends and the dog entered. Inside they found a spacious room with six tables but no customers. The moment they sat down at a table a small man appeared. He was wearing a white tunic with a black apron tied around his narrow waist and

in his thin fingers he held what appeared to be a menu. Above his long, thin upper lip, and beneath the long, thin pointy nose, rested a long, thin, pointy moustache, that quivered each time the man spoke.

'Good afternoon, good afternoon, welcome, welcome,' he said to each of them in turn. 'Such a lovely day, don't you think? Such a lovely day...'

After presenting the menu to Milly he stepped back and smiled benignly. The menu indicated that there was just one meal available, described as a stew and priced at 1 RED.

'I wonder what sort of stew it is?' mused Milly as she passed the menu round the table.

'I don't care!' said Sam, hungry enough to eat anything, whatever it was. 'It's all there is, so we'll have it!' Then looking at the waiter he said, 'We'll all have stew, please.'

The man retrieved the menu and, tucking it under his arm with a flourish, said in a deep voice, 'Three stews coming up.'

'Four stews, if you don't mind,' said Drago, jumping onto the chair at the fourth side of the table.

The waiter gazed at him for a moment, then acknowledged him with a reluctant nod of his head and said, 'Of course, slave dog, if your master agrees.'

They all nodded vigorously.

'Absolutely,' said George. 'He deserves it.'

'Very well,' said the waiter giving them a thin smile and, with a slight sniff and a flurry of moustache, turned away to fetch their order.

As soon as the food arrived, the children tucked in greedily; though used to paltry meals, they could not remember feeling this hungry in a long while. The meal, whilst tasting delicious, was a bit of a curiosity in itself. Despite having all cleared their bowls, none of them had any idea exactly what sort of meat it was they had eaten.

Drago murmured quietly, 'Nobody eats animals in Littlewich, apart from the Robes. It's not polite to ask about what you are eating, you just have to lick your lips and say something nice.'

'That was delicious,' said Milly smiling at the waiter hovering nearby. The others expressed similar sentiments, which drew a broad smile from the Minling. Turning his head, the waiter looked towards the kitchen. 'Alrina, my dear,' he called.

'Our customers are leaving.'

Immediately a small woman appeared and stood beside him. She wore a similar black apron but she was also the first Minling they had seen who was not skinny. A bright smile greeted them and little fat arms reached out to shake a greeting to each of them. 'My, oh my,' she said beaming. 'I have never seen strangers like you before. You're not Robes and you're not Minlings. Where are you from?'

They looked at each other, unsure how to respond. 'From the other side of the thorn hedge,' suggested Sam.

'No, no you can't be,' said the woman cheerfully. 'The Robes would have pegged you out by now. There are only monsters on the other side of the hedge, and you're not monsters.'

'Let's just say we have come a long, long way to visit Littlewich,' said George. Then to change the subject he added, 'Can we pay you for the meal?'

'Exactly four red leathers,' replied the woman, holding out her chubby little hand.

George dug in his pocket and pulled out three farthings and a ha'penny, which he showed to her.

'Will this cover it?' he asked, doubtfully. The tubby little woman looked at the coins with a frown, then turned her eyes back towards George.

'I said four red leathers, if you please.' Her eyebrows developed a most unwelcoming frown. At the same time, the eyes of the waiter hardened into narrow slits.

Realising this strange land had its own currency,

45

and the dull, copper coins, adorned with the Queen's head, meant nothing to the people here, George didn't know quite what to do. For a moment he just stammered in embarrassment.

'Erm... That's all we have,' he managed to say.

'Husband, call the Robes!' the woman shouted, no longer smiling, and she stamped her foot in anger.

'We'll be back to pay you later,' said Sam earnestly, grabbing George by the collar and tugging him towards the door. 'We'll get the money somehow.' Gesturing to the others, he urged them to move fast. 'We promise,' he implored, as they headed for the exit.

Startled into action, Milly and Drago followed the two boys fleeing out into the street. Unfortunately, Milly was too slow and the waiter grabbed her by the shoulder. Hearing her squeal, the boys stopped and turned around. Milly was in the doorway, struggling to escape from the waiter's clutches. He had changed his grip and now held Milly with his forearm tight against her throat. She could only gurgle and wave her arms helplessly.

It was Drago who went back to help, dragging George behind him.

'Please let her go,' George pleaded, trying to hold the dog back. 'She means no harm.'

The waiter lashed out with his foot at the grey dog and continued to shout loudly. 'Help! Thieves! Robbery!'

Several passers-by moved towards them, but then

stopped suddenly as they heard Drago snarl. His grey fur stood on end and his whole body swelled and bulged until he looked more like a ferocious lion than a dog. Waving his head from side to side, he glared at all the Minlings around him with burning red eyes. Moving slowly forward, the big dog approached the waiter and let out a long, low rumbling growl, baring his teeth for extra emphasis. With a frightened yelp the waiter released his grip around Milly's throat and the struggling girl slipped free, racing past Drago to join the two boys.

As she did so, the huge dog continued to glare and growl at the waiter. But then, seeing Milly was safe, Drago stopped growling, his fur relaxed and

his body shrank in size quite rapidly.

'I do beg your pardon, sir,' he started to apologise to the waiter. 'I'm afraid that you made me very angry and...'

'RUN Drago!' shouted Sam. 'COME ON!'

The dog turned round abruptly and chased after the others, who were now sprinting down the street as fast as they could, the angry cries of the waiter and his wife ringing in their ears.

5

THE TICK-TOCK BIRD

Having escaped the town of Littlewich without further incident, Milly, George and Sam sat by the side of the river and reviewed their position.

'We have no money,' said Sam despondently.

'We have no food,' said Milly.

'And we have nowhere to sleep tonight,' added George. 'We can't get out of this place and the Robes, whoever they are, must surely be looking for us!' He slumped down with his chin resting in his hands.

'And what's more,' said Milly, looking at the sky, 'it's getting dark.'

Drago was sitting on his haunches and looking at them anxiously. 'I know a place where we might be able to rest tonight,' he said.

'Where?' they replied in unison.

He looked towards a building further down the path. 'In the food warehouse down by the jetty. It's where the cargo boat from Dome City docks. In my brief stay there, I noticed a lot of open windows. I couldn't possibly climb through them, but I'm sure you could manage it quite easily.'

'Let's go and have a look,' said George. 'We have to spend the night somewhere.'

The path alongside the river led to a jetty and next to it, the warehouse. It was a large, plain building made of a thin, wavy metal quite unfamiliar to the children. Much to their disappointment, a guard was sitting on a chair outside the main door, though from the slump of his head, he appeared to be asleep. As they crept past him, a strange clicking noise came from overhead. Looking skywards, they saw a bird hovering just above their heads, the flapping of its wings making the curious clicking sound.

'A Tick-Tock bird,' said Drago by way of explanation. 'Nothing to worry about.'

As he spoke, the Tick-Tock bird flew down rather awkwardly and settled itself on the head of the guard, who stirred, looked up slowly and blinked. The bird had wings like a large bat, but its soft face and big eyes made it look more like a flying hamster. They stared at the strange creature standing on the guard's head as it folded its wings away.

Awake now, and aware of his small audience, the guard smiled warmly. 'Don't mind Batty,' he said cheerfully. 'She's the laziest Tick-Tock in the whole world.' He tilted his head back and Batty flapped her awkward looking wings to keep her balance.

'And this man is the laziest Minling you will ever meet, because he has the easiest job in the world,' piped up the bird in a shrill voice, ruffling her thick, black fur.

'It can talk?' said Drago, sounding surprised. To the children, talking animals appeared to be perfectly normal now. George puzzled at Drago's reaction.

The guard bit his lower lip, but said nothing.

'What is your job?' Milly asked the guard, by way of making conversation.

The guard was about to speak, but the flying hamster was quicker off the mark. 'He's supposed to guard the warehouse, but since nobody ever comes to rob the warehouse, he doesn't have very much to do.'

The guard laughed and, standing up, he offered his hand to the three friends. 'You don't look like Minlings,' he said, eyeing them up and down with an inquisitive but amiable expression. 'Who are you and what are you doing here?'

A bit taken aback by meeting a friendly person in this strange place, they all shook hands. It was Sam who answered. 'Actually, we're a bit lost and looking for somewhere to stay for the night.'

'And we don't have any money,' added Milly,

showing the guard her biggest, saddest eyes.

'He has lots of money!' the flying hamster chipped in again. 'Tell these nice people how you make lots of money, Jangle.'

'Batty, you were bad enough when you couldn't talk, but now you are impossible. You are a very naughty girl,' said the guard. But he smiled broadly as he spoke, to show that Batty hadn't offended him at all.

The Tick-Tock spread her wings and clicked them several times. 'I saw you lot,' she said. 'You were out in the grasslands when the Muttons attacked that ugly dog you have in tow.'

They all looked at Drago.

'He's not ugly! He is absolutely beautiful,' said Milly, throwing her arms around the dog's neck. 'He saved my life just now.'

Drago glared at Batty. 'And you, Tick-Tock, will be in trouble if the Robes find out you can talk,' said the dog. 'Everybody knows that Tick-Tocks can't talk.'

'They can if they flew through the Rainbow cave,' chortled Batty. 'I've been changed, and the Robes can't fly, so they can't catch me.'

'You talk too much,' said Jangle. He raised his hand and the bird hopped onto his arm. Bringing his little friend down to his lap, the Minling and the bird looked back at the newcomers.

'You won't tell the Robes about Batty, will you?' said Jangle, suddenly looking quite worried. He was a young man with an open face and thick, curly hair. He wore a ready smile and his bright blue eyes matched the blue of his jacket. Under this he wore a yellow tunic that looked slightly grubby from work. The friends took this to be the uniform of a guard.

'The cheeky bird will be pegged out if the Robes catch her,' continued Jangle. 'They hate every creature who gets changed.'

'We certainly won't tell anyone,' George answered for all of them.

'Where did you say you came from?' asked Jangle, giving them a sideways glance.

'From the other side of the big thorn hedge,' answered Sam, regretting his words as soon as he'd spoken them.

'Really?' said Jangle, tilting his head slightly. 'That's why you all look so different. But you don't look like giants.'

Sam laughed.

'That's because we're not giants. We're just normal children.'

'Still growing, then?' asked Jangle, looking at the tops of their heads, already slightly higher than his own.

'We've got a bit of growing to do,' Sam was thinking about food again. 'So long as we get enough to eat.'

Jangle nodded. 'Could be giants then, before you know it.'

George jumped in, his priorities being far more pressing.

'What we really need is a place to sleep, just for

the night.'

Jangle thought for a moment.

'Go on, Jangle,' cried Batty. 'You can put them in the Grand Suite!'

'All right,' he nodded. 'You can stay here tonight if you want. The Robes keep a very comfortable room inside, but they only use it on cargo days. We call it the Grand Suite for fun. It's not so grand, but it's not bad really. I live inside as well, so you can tell me all about the world on the other side of the hedge.'

The guard stood up and pushed a button at the side of the door. A small globe hanging over the door gave out a bright white light. The children jerked their heads up and stared at it in surprise. Milly and Sam took a step backward. The only light in Mercy Hall came from candles or the new fangled gas lights, which were quite dull in comparison to this brilliant glow. George was quite fascinated.

'Never seen an electric bulb before?' asked Jangle, smiling.

The three shook their heads dumbly.

'My, my,' said Jangle, shaking his head. Gesturing for them to enter, he added, 'Well, my work is over for the day and the night is approaching. Kindly join me inside and make yourselves comfortable.'

Just inside the entrance were four doors on either side of a corridor leading to a spacious interior packed high with boxes and crates of different shapes and sizes.

'This is the main store room,' said Jangle,

showing them around, 'where I store all the food and supplies that the Robes bring from the Dome City. I have to check it all in and note it all down in the records. The shopkeepers in Littlewich come and buy what they need, which is when I check it all out again. When the Robes come next, I give them all the money I have collected, less of course a small discount to pay for my labours.'

Batty cackled. 'He makes a fortune!' she teased. 'The Robes never bother to check the accounts, so he helps himself to anything he wants.' The bird hopped up and down and chortled some more.

Jangle gave a frown and hunched his shoulders. 'That is not true! It's a very responsible job,' he said, then smiled again. 'And you can check the accounts, if you like.'

The children shook their heads.

'Come on,' said Jangle. 'Let me show you to your room.'

Of the four rooms on either side of the corridor, one was an office stuffed full of filing cabinets from floor to ceiling, another a tiny kitchen with a stove and wash basin, the third Jangle's bedroom and the final room was the guest room for the Robes. It was a big room, very comfortable, with three beds in it and a washroom in a side alcove. It also had a bright light that came on when they flicked a button by the door.

'This is incredible,' said Milly with delight as

she looked around the room. She kept flicking the button and chuckling as the light in the middle of the room clicked on and off.

The three friends tested the beds for comfort and smiled happily. Jangle looked pleased.

'You can stay here as long as you like,' he said. 'Except of course when the Robes are coming. But don't worry about that. Batty sees them coming first, then flies in to tell me. It gives me time to prepare.' His face took on a serious look. 'If that happens, you must disappear and leave the room tidy. I don't want the Robes to know about you. They would not approve. In fact, you should avoid them at all costs... They peg out creatures they don't like.'

After settling in and getting themselves cleaned up a little, they gathered around the small table in the kitchen where Jangle proudly cooked them a meal of porridge and fruit. After the meal they sat and talked for a long time. Soon the conversation came round to the Rainbow Cave and how it could change anyone who passed through it. Jangle took a keen interest in Drago's story.

'So you've been changed in the cave, like Batty?' he said, eyes wide with interest.

'Indeed I have,' answered Drago. 'And a lot of good it's done me too.'

'Then you are also in hiding,' added the guard more soberly. 'If the Robes catch you, you're mutton feed!'

'I think it's absolutely dreadful!' exclaimed Milly, banging her small fists on the table. 'Why, it's barbaric! Why do they hate anyone who goes through the Rainbow Cave?'

Jangle shrugged his bony shoulders. 'I don't know, but they do!'

There was a long moment of silence as they thought about the Robes, the Minlings and this strange new land they had stumbled into.

'You don't have any leathers on your belts,' observed Batty, studying each of them in turn. 'How do you buy things?'

Jangle showed them some local currency. It consisted of small coloured squares of leather with a hole in the middle, which Minlings kept on a string and fastened to their belts.

'We owe four red leathers to a very angry waiter,' said Sam. 'I promised him we would return and pay him for our meal.'

'And so you shall!' piped up Batty. 'Go on Jangle, give them a string of leathers.'

Jangle winked and left the room. He returned quickly with a string of coloured leather squares long enough to nearly fit around his waist.

'Here you go,' he said, giving them to Sam. 'I have more than I need. Just don't tell anyone where you got these from,' he added with a cautious tap on the nose.

Jangle went on to tell them that the Minlings were also frightened of the Robes, but respected them as the authority in the land. There weren't many of them, at least, they were never seen in large groups, but they ruled Littlewich and its surroundings with a rod of iron, and the Minlings did everything they were told to do. When the Robes wanted someone to work in their valley, they simply took a Minling back on the cargo boat with them. No one would ever dare ask where they had gone or if they were ever coming back.

'We never see them again,' said Jangle, with a heavy shake of the head. 'Some of my best friends have disappeared.' Turning to Batty he added, 'And you, my fine flying friend, must learn to hide the fact that you have been changed by the Rainbow Cave. If the Robes find out that you can talk, you will be turned into Mutton feed too.'

'Fat chance!' laughed Batty. 'The Robes will never find out, and even if they did how could they catch me? You're forgetting I can fly. The Robes can't fly can they?' And with that, she flew up to the ceiling and circled around the room, cackling loudly as her wings tick-tocked back and forth.

'You always talk too much. In fact you never stop talking,' responded Jangle.

'How else can I acquaint you with my superior wisdom and knowledge of everything?' shouted the cheeky Tick-Tock as she circled round once more before coming to rest on the back of a chair.

'But now,' she said, folding her wings away, 'perhaps our guests might tell us a little of their life in the land beyond the hedge. I'm very eager to hear.'

'So am I,' added Jangle. 'Is that really where you come from?'

And so the three children told the sad story of their life behind the hedge, about the orphanage where they lived and how bad the food was, and how hard the work was and how cold the nights were. They told also how only human people could talk, not the animals, apart from perhaps the odd parrot, but even then not very much. Proudly they described the new railway system and the canals that transported heavy goods around the land. Sam elaborated on the exploits of the soldiers and sailors who had conquered a huge portion of the world. But when they described how man could fly up into the air, in a large balloon with a small basket tied underneath, there were snorts of derision from Batty and Jangle.

'A likely tale,' said Batty, 'You have been teasing us with impossible tales.'

'It's true!' exclaimed Milly, but Batty and Jangle howled with laughter.

'I believe you,' said Drago. 'If you say so, it must be true.' The slave dog looked at Milly with affection.

Eventually Sam, Milly and George became so tired they had to go to bed. They bid goodnight to their new friends and retired to the Grand Suite for some well-earned sleep. Drago came with them and settled himself at the foot of Milly's bed. Feeling much safer with the dog watching over her, she promptly fell into a deep, deep sleep.

6

THE TRIALS OF BATTY

Their breakfast the following morning was interrupted by an excited Batty, shrieking loudly as she flew in through an open window. 'The Robes are coming! They'll be here soon! Everyone disappear!' She flew round the room in a circle and shot back out the way she came in.

The children threw their few belongings together hastily and gathered by the main door.

'You needn't go far,' insisted Jangle. 'But keep an eye out. When it's safe to come back, I'll send you a signal.'

They walked quickly away from the warehouse and the approaching barge, which had slowly emerged from the tunnel entrance, just visible in the distance. Curiosity however, got the better of them. They hid behind a low wall, to watch the arrival of the Robes and their cargo.

A figure at the back of the barge grasped the tiller firmly and steered the vessel into the quayside. They saw Jangle tie it up to the jetty using a thick rope. Another figure emerged from a cabin on the boat and looked about, as though sniffing the air for information. Both were dressed in the same orange garments as the kidnappers from last night. It consisted of a full-length orange gown, topped with a hood that covered the face completely, apart from the slightest hint of chin. As both the newcomers disembarked and entered the warehouse with their hands clasped in front of them, they looked like medieval monks on their way to morning prayers. After they disappeared into the warehouse with Jangle, the friends resumed their journey along the path.

'I'm hungry,' announced Sam, shaking his string of coloured leathers in front of him, knowing them to mean only one thing - food! 'I say we return to that inn and pay our debts. Then, if we are gracefully received, perhaps we shall allow them to serve us with breakfast.'

'No,' said Milly indignantly. 'We need to pay for last night's meal, but I'm not going to eat there ever again. That man tried to strangle me. Who knows what he may do to our food!'

'Milly's right,' added George. 'It's too much of a risk. You go and pay the debt, Sam. Milly and I will find somewhere else for breakfast.'

'Righto,' said Sam, and headed off.

'Drago,' added Milly. 'You'd best go with him and keep him safe.'

'Must I?' groaned the dog, unwilling to face the angry waiter again.

'Please, Drago,' said Milly. 'We can't take any risks.'

'Very well then,' said the dog, and trotted off after Sam.

'It's a strange place we're in, and no mistake,' said George, as they watched their friends head towards town.

'I know,' said Milly. 'I wonder if we shall ever get out.'

George smiled. 'I'm sure we will. In fact, I know we will,' he said brightly. 'Now come on, let's find somewhere to eat.'

Milly decided they should try a cheerful looking restaurant they found, with tables and chairs set out in a pleasant garden in front of the building. The building's facade was painted a bright yellow, and red balloons floated on long strings fastened to each table.

A bright sun warmed them up and, after a short while, Sam and Drago joined them at a table, their mission complete.

'Everything go all right?' asked George, glad to see them both safe and well.

'No problem,' said Sam with a big grin. 'I put the leathers in his hand before he even recognised who I was. By the time he'd cottoned on, we were back out of the door and away up the street.'

A waitress skipped out to greet them with a broad smile. She wore a red dress with a wide yellow ribbon tied around her waist and fastened at the back in a huge bow.

'Hello customers, my name is Trixie,' she announced with a bright smile. 'Would you like a morning meal to start the day?' She was smaller than Milly and had the typical bony features of a Minling, but her face was pretty and she carried an air of cheerfulness about her.

'Indeed we would! What can you recommend?' asked George, warming to her at once.

Trixie pulled a small menu from her pocket and read it out. 'We have little fat corn crabs, oatmeal porridge with prunes, fried fish and also some strawberry jam scrumptions.'

'I could eat a horse,' laughed Sam. 'I'll have all of those things.'

Trixie took a step backwards and a deep frown appeared on her face. 'I'm afraid we do not eat horses in this town.' She looked over her shoulder and all around in case there happened to be a horse nearby that could take offence at such an outrageous comment. 'It simply isn't done!'

Sam hastened to explain. 'No, no, I don't really mean a horse! It's just something I say when I'm very hungry. No, of course we don't really eat horses either.'

'Well, if you don't do it, I suggest you don't say it!' Trixie said, brushing down her dress as if wiping away dirt. Putting her smile back in place, she motioned them to follow her. 'Come this way, please,' she said and led them to a glass tank standing on a table in front of the shop.

They gathered round and stared into the tank. Inside there were a dozen crabs standing on a bed of sand. They were quite small with eyes standing out on stalks. As the friends looked down, the crabs looked back at them, squeaking and waving their claws.

'Pick some,' invited Trixie. 'They're very tasty.'

Milly jumped back. 'I couldn't eat live crabs,' she said in horror.

'Don't be silly, we cook them first,' said Trixie with a laugh.

None of them could bring themselves to select a corn crab however, so they retreated from the tank and gave their order to the waitress.

'I think we'll stick with the porridge and prunes.' said George.

'And perhaps the fish too,' added Sam, uncertain that porridge would be enough for him.

'Followed by Strawberry Scrumtions,' said Milly, none too sure about porridge or fish. 'They sound delicious!'

'A good choice!' Trixie trilled, jotting the order in her note book, then skipped away to alert the chef.

For a while they sat in the warm sun and chatted while watching a few small boats floating up and down the slow moving river. It seemed to be a quiet, lazy day and for a while they all forgot about their situation and started to relax, and even feel quite jolly. Together they laughed over the horse misunderstanding, and wondered what a corn crab might taste like, though none of them dared try to find out.

Trixie brought the porridge and fish on a large tray and the friends found the food very much to their liking. The Strawberry Scrumptions tasted a lot like a trifle, but in addition to a topping of strawberries there were pieces of chocolate and helpings of blue ice cream, all wrapped in a sweet pastry shell.

'This is truly wonderful,' said Milly, licking her lips as she emptied her plate. Then, looking at Drago who was lying quietly at her feet, she suddenly realised the dog had avoided the food altogether.

'Drago! You haven't eaten a thing!' she cried in alarm.

The slave dog raised his head off the ground and peered up at her. 'I only eat once a day and that is in the evening.'

'But you'll starve!' Milly insisted.

'I'd rather be underfed than overfed. A little hunger sharpens the senses, don't you know?'

'Not sure I agree, old chap,' said Sam, scraping the last few crumbs from his plate. 'But each to his own I suppose.'

With all plates cleaned, they thanked Trixie and told her what a delightful meal it had been. The pretty little waitress beamed at them happily. Sam fished out his string of coloured leathers and watched in fascination as Trixie deftly removed a blue, a red and a yellow square and gave them a green one back as change.

'Goodbye, and do come again,' she said merrily as she skipped back inside.

With full stomachs and happy smiles, they left the cafe and wandered lazily back towards the centre of town. They still needed to find somebody who could tell them how to get back through the thorn hedge as it was unlikely they could hang around for much longer without getting into more trouble. It was Drago who suggested the Town Hall.

'It's full of learned types, who know about all sorts of things. You may find someone there who knows the secret of the hedge. It's worth a try, but keep me on a short lead; I won't be suspected if it's thought I have an owner.'

As they reached the centre of town, they saw a large crowd of Minlings gathered in front of the Town Hall. A Robe stood at the top of the wide steps that led up to the tall, wooden doors of the entrance. In his right hand he held up a wire cage. The friends were curious to know what was going on, so they mingled with the crowd and stayed to watch.

As they pressed through the crowd, Drago began to mumble, 'I don't like this. I don't like this at all.'

Opening the door of the cage, the man in the orange gown thrust in his free hand and pulled out a fluttering Tick-Tock bird. As the bird flapped frantically, the Robe threw it into the air. The bird flew up a short way, but was restrained by a line tethered to its feet, preventing it from making an escape. The cord tightened as the frantic bird flew from left to right, trying to get away.

'Let me go this minute!' screeched the bird to the people below. 'I demand you let me go!'

There came a loud gasp from the crowd. 'It talks!' shouted a voice in the crowd. 'The Tick-Tock talks.

It's been changed.'

The entire crowd started to grumble and mutter at once, shaking their fists at the hovering bird. A lone voice called, 'Peg it out!' and the the crowd eagerly took up the chant, 'PEG IT OUT! PEG IT OUT!'

George turned to Sam and Milly. 'It's Batty,' he declared with a look of astonishment on his face. 'It has to be.'

Drago shook his head wearily.

'I knew it. It had to happen sooner or later...'

As the chanting continued, the voice of Batty could be heard shrieking at the crowd and the Robe who had a firm hold on the cord.

'Minlings are Dunderheads and Robes are Orange Top Knots!' The shout was defiant, and the bird flapped her wings as hard as she could, but it was all to no avail. The cord held her fast and the chanting grew louder.

During the commotion, Jangle appeared, pushing himself through the crush. His face was white and the children could see he was very distressed. They drew him aside and moved away from the jeering mass to a corner where they could talk.

'I told that silly bird to stop talking time and time again,' Jangle lamented, once they were out of earshot of the crowd. 'But she just wouldn't be quiet,' he groaned, wiping a wet nose on his sleeve.

'What happened?' asked Milly.

'One of the Robes tripped over carrying some cargo off the barge and Batty was watching,' replied Jangle. 'She just laughed. The Robe stood up and said to me, 'Do you think that is funny?' I apologised, of course, hoping he would think it was me that sniggered, and that Batty would stay silent and just fly away. But no, she couldn't resist it. She laughed even louder and said, 'Very entertaining. Better if you had fallen in the river.' Then she cackled again at her own joke and flew up to the top window ledge. But the other Robe was watching from the window and grabbed her legs as she landed.' Jangle looked forlorn and tears started to run down his face. 'The Muttons will have her tonight,' he said choking back a sob.

'Not while we're here!' exclaimed Sam vehemently. 'We'll get her back!'

Jangle shook his head sadly. 'They might catch you instead. Then what?'

'Quite right,' added Drago. 'It would be bad for all of us.'

'We need a plan,' said Milly urgently. 'Come on you two, think!'

'When will they peg out Batty?' George asked Jangle.

'Very soon. The crowd will follow the Robe down to the grassland and then pull Batty down to the ground. Once the peg is in that will be the end of her.'

'Will the Robe and the crowd cross over that little bridge we used when we came into town yesterday?'

'Yes, it's the only way out.'

'Then we might have a plan!'

George pulled the other two into a huddle, explained what they needed to do, then turned back to Jangle. 'There was a boat tied up by the warehouse when we left you this morning. Do you think I could borrow it?'

'Yes, it's mine. What do you plan to do?'

'There's no time to explain. Is it easy to steer?'

'Very easy, once you get the engine going. I'll show you how.'

'Right then,' said George, looking each of them in the eye. 'You know what we have to do, so let's go!'

George hurried away with Jangle, going steadily at first so as not to attract attention, but running fast when they got to the path alongside the river.

Milly, Sam and Drago moved slowly around the crowd and walked down to the bridge over the river.

'If we manage to free Batty we have to be able to escape ourselves,' said Milly and as they crossed the bridge she looked anxiously up the river to the warehouse. 'I do hope George gets here in time.'

'Has he ever steered a powerboat before?' asked Drago, very concerned that the whole venture would turn into a disaster for them all.

'What's a 'powerboat'?' asked Sam.

Drago groaned and scratched his ear. Already he could feel the bristles on his neck rising.

A few minutes later there was a great commotion and they saw the crowd of Minlings move away from the Town Hall and begin walking down to the bridge. In the lead, the tall figure of the Robe in his orange gown loomed head and shoulders above the rest. His outstretched hand held the cord that secured the doomed Tick-Tock bird aloft.

When the crowd reached the bridge, Milly, Sam and Drago were waiting on the other side, ready to implement their plan.

'Here we go,' said Sam to the dog, winding up his lead very short.

'Good luck,' said Milly, clasping Sam's hand briefly.

As soon as the Robe started to cross the bridge, so did Sam and Drago. They walked purposefully towards the Robe until they met together in the middle. A close look at the cold features peering out from under the orange hood showed the pale, gaunt face of a man, with a beaky nose and deep set eyes. Sam had to steel himself for some extra courage, having never been this close to a Robe before. A look of surprise came over the Robe's face as he realised that a stranger blocked his way.

But it was not blocked for long.

The Robe was just about to speak when Sam turned round abruptly and ran back the way he had come, unravelling Drago's lead as he went. At the same time, Drago darted round the back of the Robe, dragging his lead behind him, and followed Sam back along the bridge. As they ran, the long lead caught the Robe behind his knees and stretched out tight. Before the Robe could step away, the lead jerked him off his feet. He cried out as he crashed over backwards and fell heavily into a crumpled heap on the bridge.

Pulling the lead away, Sam and Drago saw to their horror the Robe had managed to hold onto the cord attached to Batty. The poor bird was still captive, though she fluttered and pulled as much as she could to get away. Without hesitation, Drago dashed back into the throng and, as the Robe tried to rise, bit him firmly on the hand.

It worked.

The Robe roared in surprise and pain, loosened his grip, and the string ran free as Batty soared up into the sky. The crowd of Minlings strained their necks to watch, stunned by the sudden change in events. At first there was silence, then a great roar of rage went up from the crowd as they realised they had been cheated of the spectacle of a talking Tick-Tock bird getting pegged out for the Muttons.

With the Tick-Tock bird now little more than a dot in the sky, the Robe, clutching his hand, roared out in a hoarse voice, 'APPREHEND THE STRANGERS!'

The crowd turned its attention towards the perpetrators of the attack and began to move across the bridge. Sam, Milly and Drago were running alongside the river towards the warehouse and a small boat that was being steered towards them.

With a great surge the Minlings chased after them, led by the seething Robe. The long skinny legs of the pursuers allowed them to move surprisingly quickly. When Sam glanced over his shoulder, he was shocked to see them gaining so rapidly.

'Faster!' he screeched at Milly and, as she was running in front of him, he gave her a little push between the shoulders. Throwing her head back, she summoned deep reserves of energy to carry her faster along the path.

George found the powerboat to be much slower than he had hoped. Jangle had started it for him, shown him how to set the speed and steer in a straight line. He had mastered it quite well, despite never having been in a boat before, but now he wanted speed.

He watched with baited breath as his friends raced down the bank towards towards the water's edge, with the Robe and the Minlings in hot pursuit. A shiver of fear ran down his spine when he saw that Milly and Sam were close to being captured. If they were, there was no way he'd be able to rescue them all on his own.

Running alongside the fleeing pair, Drago also realised that the rescue boat was not going fast enough to meet them in time.

'You go on!' he called to Milly and Sam. 'I'll hold them off!'

Skidding to a sudden halt, he turned to face the approaching crowd.

Lowering his head to the ground, the slave dog splayed his front legs apart, dug his claws into the soft soil and growled. The hairs on his back stood on end, his eyes glowered red with a deep, inner

rage. No Minling was going to hurt Milly and her friends while Drago was around. The dog's body swelled, his snarling and growling grew louder too. To anyone watching, it was a fearsome sight to behold.

The Robe slowed, hesitating, unsure of whether he ought to try to pass Drago or not. As he came to a stop, all the Minlings around him stopped as well. The Minlings at the rear crashed headlong into those at the front. Piling up on top of each other, their cries and shouts and wails rose up into the air. Before the seething mass could sort itself out, Drago had turned away and was racing after Milly and Sam.

The boat was nearing the bank of the river now. George gave a great cheer for Drago and called out encouragement to his friends. 'Come on Sam, jump in! Milly, run!'

Sam grabbed Milly by the hand and pulled her so quickly that she nearly fell. George swung the boat round and scraped along the bank at the side of the river. It was just near enough to allow Sam and Milly to jump on board and collapse in a heap in the bottom of the boat. Moments later, Drago, who had resumed his normal size, leapt aboard as well and landed on top of them. While they all scuffled around on the floor of the boat, George pushed off from the bank just in time to get into mid stream before the Minlings arrived.

With all the extra weight, the boat travelled even slower now. George gunned the engine as hard as he could in an effort to squeeze out every last drop of power.

Before long, a great crowd had amassed on both banks of the river. As the boat moved slowly forwards, the crowd walked with them, shouting insults and threats to the friends and throwing sticks and stones at them. The companions sat low in the boat, peering over the side and wondering what to do next.

'Come on in!' called out one Minling. 'We want to have a pegging-out party!'

'You're not one of us. You're different!' cried another. 'You've been changed.'

'Peg them out,' came the cry, that steadily turned into a chant. 'PEG THEM OUT! PEG THEM OUT!'

A few missiles managed to hit the boat, but most landed in the water with a harmless plop. Still, the children were scared. There was no way they could land on either side of the river and no chance of sailing faster than the following crowd.

'How do we get out of this one?' asked Sam, covering Milly with his arms. 'We're like sitting ducks!'

'I'll think of something,' said George, who was trying very hard, but could think of nothing that would help. He clutched the tiller firmly and steered the small boat upstream against a gentle current. Ahead of them the cliffs loomed nearer, and he realised if they didn't land soon, they would have to follow the river into the great hole in the cliffs.

'Drago,' he called. 'What's up ahead?'

Drago looked over the prow of the boat and groaned.

'We're heading towards the cave - the Rainbow Cave,' he told them with a heavy voice. 'The river carries on through and on to Dome City on the other side. We shouldn't go there if we can help it.'

'We must turn round and go back,' said George desperately. 'At least then we'll be heading downstream and we can go much faster. The Minlings are sure to get tired eventually and leave us alone.'

'Good idea,' agreed Milly. 'I certainly don't want to visit the Dome City. And we're going further away from the hedge.'

As George began to turn the boat, a yellow cord dangled down from above. Looking up they saw Batty fluttering down towards them. They clapped their hands and cheered. It was nice to see the cheeky bird they had saved from the Muttons, but the roars from the bank grew louder.

'The Tick-Tock's back!'

'Get more stones!'

Folding her wings, Batty dropped down into the boat, a serious expression on her face. 'I have been a very silly Tick-Tock bird, very silly indeed. I don't deserve such good friends.'

'Nonsense Batty,' said Sam. 'We're so glad you are safe and sound. Perhaps in future you will be more careful.'

'Luckily all Tick-Tock birds look alike, so as long as I don't talk too much, nobody will recognise me. Now, perhaps someone will undo this dreadful string and take it off my foot.'

Milly obliged, and Batty hopped to the middle of the boat.

'Why are you turning?' she barked at George.

'We're going to go back down river,' explained George to Batty. 'It's faster and...'

'You can't do that!' shrieked the bird. 'There are

ten more boats coming this way!'

'Ten?' cried Sam.

'At least! The Robes are coming to get you. And the angry Minlings too!'

'What are we to do?' cried Milly.

'You must go up river into the caves and hide inside until it's safe to come out,' said Batty. 'There are plenty of inlets where you can shelter in the dark, but you must be very quiet. And don't go too far in or you'll end up in the lake.'

'Which lake?' asked George.

'There's a big lake in there. It's where the rainbow glows. Try to avoid it if you can, or you may get changed.'

A stone whizzed over and hit the inside of the boat, making them all jump.

Batty huffed. 'Bad shot!' she called out, then turning back to the others said, 'The Minlings won't go through into the caves, they'll be too frightened, so you'll be all right. Just stay clear of the lake.'

The children looked at each other, each seeing the fear in the other's eyes. 'We have to do what Batty says,' said George at last. 'You know what will happen to us if we get caught!'

'If you don't mind, I think I'll stay outside and wait for you,' said Batty, spreading her wings and giving them a couple of beats. 'I've been through the Rainbow Cave once already, and I'd rather not do it again.'

George corrected his turn and steered the boat back upstream. The cliffs loomed nearer. On the banks of the river, the crowd, though still following, had given up the shouting and throwing of sticks, having instead grown curious to see what would happen next. As the black hole of the cave entrance widened before them, Batty stretched her wings and said, 'Well, we showed those Robes and Minlings a thing or two, eh? They won't mess with Batty the Talking Tick-Tock bird again.'

'You watch your beak, Bird!' hissed Drago through clenched teeth. 'We may not be there to help you next time.'

Batty shivered, flapped her wings and rose a little into the air.

'I think I will leave you now. I'm going to roost up on the cliffs and watch out for your return.'

Behind them, the roar of engines signalled the approach of the pursuit boats. Batty rose higher into the air.

'Goodbye, and good luck!'

'Goodbye,' they all cried, and waved to the bird as she flew higher and higher.

A roar of rage came from the watching Minlings who shook their fists at the bird and then roared again as the little boat sailed gently into the cave. George couldn't resist waving to the angry faces as they disappeared from view and the roars became little more than an echo.

'It's dark in here,' said Sam, as they moved

deeper into the gloom.

'And cold,' added Milly, wrapping the blanket tight around her shoulders.

'But at least it's safe,' said George, hoping to cheer them both a little. 'Isn't that right, Drago?'

'Oh, yes,' said the dog, without much conviction. 'Quite safe... For now.'

7

THE RAINBOW CAVE

As their eyes got used to the dark they saw a wide tunnel ahead. The light from the entrance of the cave grew fainter and fainter as they travelled deeper into the darkness. So as not to draw attention to themselves, George cut the engine and reached for a paddle to propel the boat forward. Sam reached for the other paddle and together they glided the boat silently forward.

A couple of times they bumped the boat against the side of the tunnel and either George or Sam would push it away from the walls with an oar or by hand. The stone walls were wet and slimy and the air grew steadily colder as they travelled on.

'Where do you suppose this rainbow cave is then?' asked Sam in a quavering voice.

'We should come to it soon,' said Drago. He was sitting upright in the front of the boat and staring into the darkness ahead. 'When I came through last time, they had me down below, covered in blankets. But I did sneak out for a while, unnoticed. I remember bright lights and a lot of flashing colours. That must have been when I got changed.'

'Quiet!' ordered George. 'I can hear something.'

They listened intently. From behind them came

the sound of voices.

'There's a boat following us!' said Sam in a loud whisper. 'Can't we go any faster?'

Milly put her hands over her eyes and started to sob quietly.

'I can see a light ahead,' called out Drago.

They all stared into the darkness and sure enough there was a glimmer of light in the distance. The noise from the boat behind got louder, as it got nearer, and the light ahead got brighter, as it came closer. Suddenly the tunnel widened and they sailed out onto a lake. George pulled on the tiller and they followed the wall around to the left, hoping they would soon be too far away for the boat behind them to see which way they had gone.

As they sailed further on, they became aware of a very light mist that seemed to drop down from above. It was patchy and they kept sailing in and out of it.

'This is good,' said George. 'The Robes in the boat behind will have a job finding us in this mist.'

He was right. Even when they strained very hard to listen, there was no sound of the voices they'd heard in the tunnel.

'Lets follow the wall all the way round and eventually we should find a way out,' suggested Sam.

The others agreed but after a few minutes they passed through a bank of the clinging mist and lost contact with the wall. Whichever way George steered the boat after that he could not find the wall again. Emerging from another patch of mist they looked around. In every direction there was water and wisps of mist. They were well and truly lost with no idea of which direction to steer the boat. The light, however, was bright and looking up, there was a high, thick blanket of white mist that stretched like an endless ceiling in every direction.

'Keep steering in the same direction,' said Milly

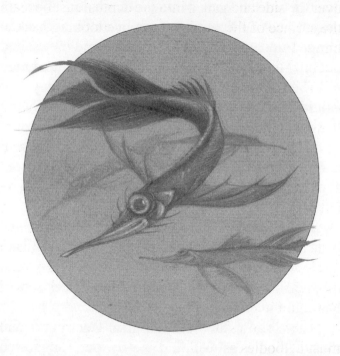

earnestly. 'That way we must eventually hit a wall.'

George decided the best way to steer in a straight line was to tie the tiller tightly so it couldn't move. He had just finished lashing it to the seat, using the string from Batty's foot, when Milly screamed.

They all jerked round to look at her. Standing bolt upright in the centre of the boat, she was pointing into the water along the side and screaming again and again.

'Hush!' said a very alarmed Sam as he reached over and pulled her down onto a seat. 'What is it?'

There was no response from Milly, she just stared and pointed at the water. Sam leaned cautiously over the side and gazed into the depths. Just beneath the surface of the water was an eye looking back at him.

Recoiling from the edge, Sam looked at George.

'There's an eye in the water and it's staring at us!' he stammered.

Hesitantly, George also looked over the side and, after studying the water for a few moments, said calmly, 'There's more than one eye in the water... There are hundreds of them.'

Sam, Milly and Drago peeped cautiously over the edge of the boat again and sure enough, they saw eyes everywhere. It seemed that more and more were appearing all the time. As the boat moved moved forward, it became clear the eyes were moving with them.

'There can't just be eyes,' said George. 'There must be bodies as well.'

'I can't see any,' said Sam. Then, peering once again over the side at the moving eyes, he exclaimed, 'You're right, there are little bodies and tails behind the eyes. It looks like tiny fish, each with one big eye.'

They drifted on and the eyes stayed with them.

A short while later they became aware of a humming noise and the light slowly changed to a pink colour that got brighter and brighter and redder and redder until the lake, the boat, and the mist were bathed in a bright red glow.

'Gosh,' said Milly, looking at the other's faces. 'We're red all over.'

But then the red light turned to orange. No sooner had they got used to the orange colour than it turned again to yellow, then green. A few minutes later everything was coated in blue.

'What's going on?' said George, looking all around him. 'Where are the colours coming from?'

'It's like being inside a rainbow...' said Milly, gazing at the light.

'A rainbow in a cave?' added Sam, frowning.

The blue remained for quite a while, gradually brightening up until it became a soft, pale blue. It reminded Milly of a warm sunny day, staring out to sea with a bright sky overhead. Her thoughts were disturbed by a bright flash in front of her eyes, followed by a deep rumble of thunder somewhere high in the roof of the cave.

Everyone dived down to the bottom of the boat and put their hands over their ears and shut their eyes tight. They yelled and shouted with fright as the lightning and the thunder crashed and crackled all around them. It was only when the colour of the light changed to violet that it became quiet again and they sat up and looked around. They were still in the middle of the lake with a violet mist hanging all around them, hovering over the water.

Soon the colours faded completely and the cave, and everything in it, appeared to have returned to normal.

'Thank goodness that's all over,' gasped Sam.

'It was amazing,' said Milly, who had now recovered from the frightening experience. Having survived the thunderstorm, she felt much better and even a little bit excited.

George looked over the side. 'The eyes are still with us,' he said.

But Sam had seen something else.

'What's that?' said Sam, pointing a quivering finger into the depths of the cave.

They all looked intently. Coming towards them on the surface of the lake they saw a black triangle, slicing through the water leaving a wash and small waves in its wake.

'Could it be a shark?' asked Milly in a voice that suddenly quavered, as she felt frightened again.

'Oh dear,' said George. 'It certainly looks like one.'

They sat and quivered in fearful anticipation as the triangle neared the boat. It was easy now to see a long sleek body gliding under the water, it's tail flapping powerfully to drive it forward. It circled the boat as if looking for a weak point to attack, then rolled over onto its back and slid under the boat. As it did so, they all saw the smooth white belly and huge mouth, half open to reveal two rows of glistening, spiked teeth.

With baited breath, the friends waited until the beast reappeared on the other side of the boat and leaped half out of the water before splashing back down and diving out of sight. The great hoard of one-eyed fish became very agitated and the surface of the water appeared to boil as they flapped closer to the top, making a noise like a waterfall.

'I'm frightened,' said Milly.

'So am I,' chorused the other two together.

'Hold tightly to the seats,' ordered George. 'That shark might try to get to us.' He stood up and took a step forward to join Milly and Sam who were huddled together in the middle of the boat.

At that moment the shark decided to attack.

A huge bang from underneath lifted the boat half out of the water. For a very long moment the boat shot forward on the back of the shark before sliding off sideways and splashing back into the water, which cascaded in as one side dipped briefly under the surface. The boat rocked violently back and forth for a while, before gradually settling down. Sam and Milly clutched the seat in the middle. Drago wedged himself under the same seat with his head under his paws.

But it was George, who had been standing upright when the shark attacked, who was now in trouble. Unable to find anything to grab hold of, he struggled to keep his balance and staggered backwards. When water came over the side, he slipped and, before anyone could reach him, fell overboard.

Sam screamed. Milly screamed. They both leaned over to pull him back, but could only watch in helpless horror as George sank below the surface.

'George!' cried Milly, but it was no use; he could not hear them.

And then, one by one, the one-eyed fish closed in. In seconds he was surrounded by hundreds of them. They attached themselves to him until no part of his body could be seen from the boat, only a great ball of swirling eyes that rolled over and over as more and more of the big eyed creatures joined the mix. The great mass of fish, with George swallowed in amongst them, moved away from the boat and dropped down into the depths of the lake.

Following on behind, its tail thrashing violently, was the shark...

There was silence. The boat bobbed on the surface as the water became still. Milly and Sam looked at each other in stunned bewilderment.

The boat drifted on through the water, further and further away from the point where their friend had disappeared. The minutes past, long and slow.

'He's been under the water for too long now,' said Sam eventually, his voice cracked with sorrow. 'He must have drowned.'

It was Drago who tried to raise their spirits.

'Not necessarily,' he said calmly. 'There is a chance...

Milly looked at him hopefully. 'What do you

mean?'

'This is the Rainbow Cave,' continued the dog. 'Strange things always happen here.'

A swishing noise from behind the boat caused them all to turn as one. Like a cork popping out of a bottle, George reappeared. He came from under the surface with both arms stretched out over his head like a diver starting a race. He bobbed in the water for a while then, spotting the boat, swam a very powerful crawl right up to it. Without stopping, he put both hands on the side and heaved himself out of the water in one quick movement.

'George!' cried Milly. 'You're alive!'

'Wow,' said Sam in surprise. 'I didn't know you could swim like that!'

Although George was dripping wet, Milly threw her arms around him and hugged him so tightly he had trouble breathing.

'Hold on, Milly,' he laughed. 'I'm fine. You can let me go.'

He jumped into the boat and sat down on the narrow bench with a relaxed sigh. Drago looked at him through narrowed eyes.

'You've been changed!' he said at last. 'I can tell.'

Milly and Sam sat backwards and looked at George afresh.

'He looks the same to me!' said Sam.

'And me,' agreed Milly. 'But maybe his shoulders are a bit bigger.'

'What happened out there?' asked Sam. 'You

were under water for ages, or did you pop up to take a breath? If you did, we didn't see you.'

'It's astonishing!' their friend replied, his face stretched by a huge grin. 'When all those eyes swarmed around me, I thought I was going to die. They seemed to kiss me with little mouths, hundreds of them. Then I started turning over and over and more and more of the eye fish covered me until I couldn't see anything at all, and just when I thought my lungs would burst, I found I could breath under water. I knew instantly I'd been changed. Then I realised the eye fish were helping me. All that kissing and clinging was to hide me from the shark.' George paused for breath. In spite of his ordeal, he was laughing and cheerful.

'What happened to the shark?' asked Sam with a snigger. It was such a relief to see George fit and well, that he couldn't help laughing with him.

'He followed us for a while, always keeping his distance. After a while, the eye fish drifted away from me and I swam around alone, watching the shark. Then the eye fish gathered again in a great crowd next to me and started to swim towards him. As they got close, the great beast just swam away. I think it was frightened of them. If they wanted to, they could have swarmed all over the shark and probably suffocated it. They may be small, but when they get together they have a power all their own. And they saved my life. What an experience!'

When he had finished speaking, Milly said, 'I wonder if I've been changed too. Do I look any different?'

The others studied her for a moment. Sam shook his head slowly. 'No, I don't think so, you look the same as always.'

'It's possible,' said Drago. 'I didn't feel my change at first. Only later, when I needed it.'

'What about me?' asked Sam. 'Am I any

different?'

'Not obviously,' replied Milly. 'But then, how could we tell? George doesn't look so different.'

While he listened to his friends speculate on whether they had been changed or not, Drago positioned himself in the prow of the boat. He was keeping a close watch on the lake ahead and was the first to spot the wall of the cave coming up in front of them.

'We're on the other side of the lake,' he called out to the others.

'At last!' they cried, and George rapidly untied the string that held the tiller in place and sat down ready to steer the boat along the wall of the lake.

'Which way shall we go?' he asked.

'These are strange waters,' said the dog, staring hard at the water flowing around the boat. 'Both rivers flow out of the mountain, as if the lake is their source.

'How does that work?' asked Sam, very confused.

'I do not know,' replied Drago. 'But it would be best to get into the current and flow with it.'

'Then that's what we'll do,' said George, as he heaved on the tiller and turned the boat into the stream.

8

THE WELCOME INN

Slowly they glided alongside the cave's edge, now and again pushing at the slimy walls to keep the boat from scraping the jagged rock.

'I see a tunnel!' cried Sam.

Ahead, he had spotted light shining into the cave. George turned the boat into the tunnel that led to the outside world and a broad river. Not a living soul was waiting for them. The boat floated gently along the river and finally the friends were able to relax a little.

'We need a plan,' said George. 'We've escaped from Littlewich, but what do we do next?'

'Well, I'm hungry,' said Sam, who liked to have at least three large meals a day. More, if he could get it.

'We should find somewhere to hide the boat in case our pursuers follow us out of the cave,' suggested George. 'Then we can forage around for some food.'

'But how are we going to get back to the hedge?' asked Milly, fearing they may find themselves unable to return home.

'I've no idea,' said George. 'But right now we need to eat.'

'I couldn't agree more,' added Sam, rubbing a hand over his rumbling tummy.

The river moved sluggishly through open countryside. Plenty of trees leaned over the water's edge, dipping their lower branches into the water. A few logs floated on the surface and small fish could be seen swimming around the boat. Sudden scuffles at the water's edge revealed small mammals scurrying about in the undergrowth.

The banks grew steeper as they moved on. When a particularly large willow tree cascaded its branches and leaves across the water, Sam suggested they moor the boat under the tree where it would be out of sight while they explored. As they turned for the bank, one of the floating logs opened its mouth and yawned.

'Yikes!' cried Sam in surprise. 'A crocodile!'

They stared in horror as what they had thought was a log turned with a swish of its mighty tail. Raising its head above the water, it adjusted its position and glided straight towards them.

'Back, back to the other bank,' Sam shouted to George. But his friend had already seen the danger and was hurriedly steering the boat away from it.

'No!' shouted Milly. 'There's another one over there. Look!' Sure enough, another huge beast, with its mouth stretched open, was coming towards them from the other side. They realised that the logs surrounding them had all been sleeping crocodiles. But now those crocodiles were awake, and very hungry.

'I'm going for the willow tree,' shouted George, hoping he would be able to beat the crocodiles in a race to the bank.

There were only a few yards to go when the first crocodile put on a spurt and, raising its huge snout above the side of the boat, opened its gaping mouth. Rows of teeth bristled before them, and foul breath assaulted their nostrils and lungs. As the creature lunged, it headed straight for where Milly was sitting. However, instead of screaming, she clenched her fist, pulled back her skinny arm, and punched the crocodile right on its nose. The punch was so strong, her arm was a blur as it hit the animal's snout. The result was startling. The crocodile recoiled and dived away in alarm.

Before it could recover its wits, George drove the boat into the bank next to the willow tree. The four of them leapt out and slithered up the steep and muddy bank. Their feet sunk into the sticky mud and they had to scrabble on all fours to escape.

George was the first to make it to the top of the bank, with Sam close behind. But Milly's feet got stuck in the mud and she stumbled forwards. Drago turned around to help her. As she struggled to pull her feet out of the clinging mud, the angry dog came alongside her, his hairs already beginning to bristle as they had done so many times before. A deep growl gurgled out of his throat as he prepared to fight to save Milly. This time however, he was facing a fight he could not win. Several huge crocodiles were now padding out of the river, keen to take part in the anticipated meal on the riverbank. To them, a dog, no matter how big and angry, would be no match at all.

As George and Sam watched, helpless, they were astonished to see Milly coming to the rescue of Drago. Dragging her feet free from the mud, she flung herself at the crocodile with her fists flailing. Encouraged by her first punch, she did it again. And again! The huge animal turned its head away in pain as a tiny but deadly fist hit it square on its nose. Then it tried to sweep her back into the water by swishing its tail round in a deadly circle. Milly saw it coming and, stepping back, grabbed the flailing tail by its tip. Keeping a tight grip on the scales she pulled hard. To everyone's amazement, the crocodile stopped in its tracks.

Lifting the tail as high as she could with both hands, she brought them down again in the way one would crack a whip. The crocodile's whole body jerked up and down and its head banged onto the ground. It heaved its tail free from Milly's hands and slithered back into the river as fast as it could.

Before any more of the beasts could attack them, Milly and Drago turned and ran to join the boys at the top of the bank.

'My goodness!' cried Sam. 'You have been changed. You're as strong as a bear! What happened?'

'I don't know,' replied Milly. She held her hands out in front of her, staring at the small, dainty fingers. 'When I saw the crocodile open its jaw right in front of me, I suddenly felt very strong. I knew I just had to punch the wretched thing. So I did. I could hardly believe it myself.'

'How do you feel now?' asked George, who was still in a state of shock at Milly's new found power.

'Normal, I just feel normal.'

'Can you lift George off the ground?' asked Sam.

Wrapping her arms around George's waist she heaved upwards. Nothing happened, George stayed firmly on the ground.

Drago said, 'It must be like my power; it only works when you need it.'

'It's not fair,' grumbled Sam. 'Everyone's got a new power except me.'

'Not everyone gets changed when they pass though the Rainbow Cave,' added Drago with a shrug. 'But you might have a new power yet, you just don't know what it is.'

Looking very crestfallen, Sam frowned.

'Maybe, but I can't think what it could be. Drago and Milly get very strong and George can breathe under water.' He sighed in exasperation. 'Even if I have got something, I may never notice. What then?'

'Come on,' said George. 'Let's hide the boat. The Robes might appear at any moment. They are bound to be coming this way.'

Checking the river for crocodiles, they were glad to find none in sight. They slid down the bank and dragged the boat under the cover of the willow tree and covered it with fallen branches and leaves to better conceal it. Then they climbed back up the bank and looked around. In the distance, the cliffs they had just passed through loomed high above them.

'Funny isn't it?' said George, looking at the cave mouth they had come through. 'Both this river and the other one flow out of the mountain. Neither of them flow in.'

'The lake must be the source of both rivers then,' said Milly.

'I'm hungry,' said Sam. 'We still haven't found anything to eat!'

To their right, there appeared to be a road not far away and on it a long, low building had a chimney with smoke drifting high in a windless sky. Sam's eyes brightened at the sight.

'That smoke means a fire, and a fire on a warm day like this surely means someone is cooking something, and whatever that something is, I would like to share it with them,' said Sam, rubbing his hands in eager anticipation.

'Maybe it's an inn,' suggested George.

'Then let's go and explore,' said Milly cheerfully, and showing a new found confidence, strode off in the lead. Looking at each other, the boys smiled and followed with a hopeful spring in their step.

Drago sniffed.

'Out of the frying pan...' he said to himself, and followed on behind at a steady trot.

It was an inn; an old rambling building with a barn to one side. A sign hung down over an open door. On it, the words 'THE WELCOME INN' were written in large, gold letters.

Outside two horses were tied up at a rail and two chariots, similar to the one they had seen in Littlewich, were parked to the side of the road in front of the inn. A stooped figure they took to be an old man stood on the front step, sweeping a broom from side to side with a strange jerky motion. As they got nearer they could see it was in fact a boy about their own age. The stoop was caused by him having a lump on his back and a drooping shoulder to accompany it. Thick black hair flopped forward to his eyebrows and he used powerful arms to sweep vigorously with his home made broom.

The sweeping stopped when they got close and the sound of their footsteps made him look up at them with his one good eye. The other remained half closed. An instant smile lit up his face.

'Greetings young strangers,' he said, making a half bow and an elaborate sweep with his left arm. 'Welcome to the Welcome Inn.' He pointed to the sign above his head. 'May your stay here bring you great comfort and good fortune.'

It was a pleasant greeting and Milly was the first to respond. 'Thank you, we are hoping that a good meal can be obtained at your inn.'

'Indeed it can, just step through the door and my parents will attend to your every wish.' He gestured to the open door, then looked closely at them, a slight frown crossing his face. His lazy eye twitched and he cleared his throat before adding in a lower tone, 'Perhaps you should sit close by the door. We have a couple of... "gentlemen" in the alcove at the back who might query your young appearance and the delightful way you speak. By the way, my name is Scorpio and I, personally, am *very* pleased to meet you.'

After introducing themselves in return, they entered the inn cautiously and made for the table nearest the door. Across the large room, hunched over a table tucked under an arch, sat two Robes. The children hesitated on seeing them, but the Robes, concentrating as they were on their soup and bread rolls, didn't even look up to assess the new arrivals.

'What if they see us?' said Sam nervously, looking round the room.

'They're bound to,' said George, weighing up the situation carefully. 'The question is, do they know who we are? If they do...'

'Then they'll be onto us like a shot,' said Sam, looking at the door and wondering if they should leave now. 'What then?'

'That would make me very angry,' whispered Milly sweetly in his ear. 'And I should have to punch them both on the nose.' She took a seat, sighed contentedly and added, 'I rather like this change. I can't wait to get back home, as I am not in the least bit frightened of Old Barking Mad any more.'

The boys smiled at Milly's newfound confidence and joined her at the table. Sam turned his chair outwards, ready to bolt at any second should he need to. Drago, having chosen to play the obedient pet, settled down by the door and kept a keen eye on the world outside.

Several of the other tables in the room were occupied by people who looked similar to the Minlings, but they only gave a passing glance at the newcomers and carried on with their meals and muttered conversations. A tubby little lady wearing a white apron came fussing across the room to their table, wiping her hands on a red dishcloth she kept tucked under her apron ties.

'Good day, good day, you're very welcome, pleased to see you, today we have home made pie followed by crab apples pickled in raspberry sauce for dessert.'

They would have liked to ask what was in the pie, but, remembering their previous experience, nobody did. When it came down to it, they were so hungry they didn't care. They accepted the food gratefully and asked for a few glasses of lemon pop to accompany it. When it arrived, hot and steaming in a wide bowl, surrounded by fresh potatoes and green beans, it looked delicious. And when they ate, they found it tasted as good as it looked. The crab apple and raspberry dessert, sweet and tangy at the same time, rounded the meal off perfectly.

Afterwards, Sam handed over the strip of leathers to the lady they assumed was Scorpio's mother. She gave a kindly smile, removed three red discs and, after thanking them for their custom, moved rapidly on to another table.

A poke in the back made George jump and, looking round, he saw the top end of a broom sticking out of the doorway.

'Pssst,' came a hissing noise followed by Scorpio speaking in a loud whisper. 'I'm not allowed inside during meal times,' he said by way of explanation. 'But I think you need to leave the inn rapidly by the back door. I'll meet you outside.'

Sam quickly led the way to a half open door at the back of the room. They stepped outside into a yard that stretched down to a grassy area, where a few chickens pecked vigorously at the soil. Moments later Scorpio sidled round the corner with a look of concern on his face.

'A crowd of Robes are coming! They'll be here in a few minutes,' he said and cast a worried look over his shoulder. 'They're in a hurry and coming from the same direction from which you arrived. It occurred to me that you may well have fallen foul of our revered leaders already.'

They looked at each other in despair, and George nodded despondently at Scorpio, who peered at them from under the thick black hair that flopped over his forehead.

'Follow me. We must get under cover before they arrive.' With an unsteady, loping gait he hustled them into the barn.

Inside four small horses chewed hay out of a manger. All their heads turned round together to look curiously at the three children who gathered round Scorpio.

Handing the children some lumps of sugar, he whispered, 'Give the horses these titbits and make friends with them quickly. You will have to persuade them to take you away from here. Are the Robes chasing you?'

They all nodded together.

'I thought so. They often bring strange children to the inn, then they take them to work in the Dome. You looked as though you might have escaped from them,' Scorpio stepped back and looked at them in admiration. 'You are brave,' he said. 'All the children who stay here overnight are usually frightened and want to go home. I try to be friendly with them. Sometimes they leave letters with me.'

'Letters?' asked Milly. 'What sort of letters?'

'Letters they have written.'

Milly was immediately interested. 'What do you do with them?' she asked, thinking they might be able to follow the mail out of this strange land and back through the hedge.

'Nothing really,' said Scorpio sadly. 'I can't read, my parents can't read. Only some of the Robes can read. I always take them and hope I meet someone going back the way they came.'

'We are definitely going back the way we came,' stated Milly with conviction.

The little hunchback brightened up. 'Maybe you can take them,' he said hopefully.

'Of course,' chipped in George. 'We'd be pleased to.'

Scorpio peered out of the doorway. 'You'll have to stay here until we know what the Robes are up to. I'll go and tend to them and, while you wait, you can look at the letters I've saved. They're all in the top drawer.' He pointed to a large oak chest of drawers in the corner of the stable, then sidled out through the doorway.

George pulled the drawer open. Inside was a pile of dusty pieces of paper. None had an envelope. Most were just hastily scrawled notes on a scrap of paper. George took the pile out and began to sift through it, handing some pieces to Milly and Sam. The first words they read sent chills down their spines.

'...men dressed in orange pulled me through the hedge. I don't know where I am.'

'...if you get this letter, please find us. We've been stolen...'

'...we are lost. They do not tell us where we are going...'

All three of them felt a burning rage start to well up from deep inside their hearts.

'They've been kidnapped!' said Milly.

'By the Robes,' added Sam. 'All of them...'

Suddenly George gave a stifled shout.

'Milly! This is for you!' He held out a letter which was neatly folded and had Milly's name on the front.

Looking up with shock, Milly stared at him for a moment, then snatched the letter from his outstretched hand. Trembling from head to toe, she unfolded the letter and began to read.

'It's from Tom!' she cried.

'What does it say?' asked Sam.

Milly read aloud.

'Dear Milly,
Don't know if you will get this letter, but I have to write it. The hunchback boy said he can deliver a letter. He seems honest enough so he might do it too. I never got to London. After leaving the orphanage I waited for the stage coach, but it never came. But the hedge opened, I don't know how, and two men dressed in orange threw a sack over my head. I was tied up and kept like that for hours. It was a strange journey that brought me to this place. It is a strange land I'm in and I don't know where I am or why I am here. If you get this letter beware of men dressed in orange. I hope to see you when I can escape, but I don't know where I'm going or anything about this place. Nothing is right here. Please tell someone. I have to go now, there is no time to write any more...'

Milly could hardly get the last words out. Tears filled her eyes and her bottom lip began to tremble so much, she had to bite it. George put a comforting hand on her shoulder.

'Cheer up, old girl,' he said warmly. 'If he's here,

we'll find him.'

Sam punched a fist into a palm and growled. 'Those wretched Robes. I'd like to show them a thing or two...'

Scorpio raced back into the barn carrying three small sacks and handed them to the friends. 'You must leave soon,' he said looking frightened. 'I told the Robes you had been here, had a meal, then returned to the river. They plan to return to the river in order to chase and catch you, but I persuaded them to stay for a bite to eat. 'It's tiring work, tracking down strays,' I told them.'

'Good work,' said George. 'That should give us enough time to get clear.'

'This letter is from my brother!' exclaimed Milly. 'When did you see him? How did he look? Where was he going? Why was he kidnapped?' her voice was incredulous and her eyes stared fixedly at Scorpio.

'I don't know which one he was. There's been so many pass through...' said Scorpio, keen to help, but taken aback by the intensity of Milly's questions.

'His name is Tom! Was there ever anyone called Tom?'

Scorpio shrugged. 'Might have been, maybe...'

'Where is he? Where did they take him?'

Scorpio stood in the doorway and shook his head. 'Like I said, they go the Dome.'

Milly's voice was becoming desperate.

'What for?'

Scorpio looked anxiously over his shoulder. 'I'm

sorry, but you must leave now. There is no more time to explain!'

'I must know where Tom is?' exclaimed Milly, 'And we are not going anywhere until I know!'

'They all go to work in the engine room in the big city,' said Scorpio looking up at Milly nervously. 'It's in the Dome.'

'Why?'

'I think it's because the Robes think them very able. They can read and write words. Minlings don't read or write much. Only some of the Robes can read and write. It is very hard you know and only clever people go to the engine room.'

A noise outside suddenly shocked them into silence and they listened to the voices of people talking. Scorpio grabbed his broom and started sweeping in the doorway and gradually he disappeared in the direction of the chatter.

Above the noise outside one voice spoke loudly. 'You boy, if you have lied to us, we'll be back and I'll see you're pegged out before nightfall.'

Sam had found a crack in the wall of the barn and peeping through it he saw the back of Scorpio, who stood with a broom dangling in his hand as he watched four Robes in their floating carts driving back towards the river.

The hunchback returned looking anxious, his normal cheerful smile replaced by a deep frown that creased his face. 'They've gone, but they won't be long. If they don't find you, they will peg me out for sure.' He slumped to the floor, his head dropping into his hands. 'Oh dear, what have I done?'

'You must come with us,' said George trying to cheer him up and make him feel welcome. 'We are going to the city and you are welcome to join us.'

'I'll only slow you down.'

'Don't you have a horse?' asked Sam.

Scorpio's face brightened as he began to see a way of escape.

'There is no time to waste,' he said with renewed excitement. 'I'll introduce you to the horses and we'll set off straight away.'

He limped to the four horses who were munching hay in the stables at the back of the barn. 'This is Georgehorse,' he said, reaching up with his long arm and tickling the horse behind the ear. 'A horse always has the name of the person who is riding him,' he said by way of explanation, then moved to the smallest horse and again tickled it behind the ear. 'This is Millyhorse,' he said.

The horse jerked his head up and looked hard at Milly. 'Good,' it said. 'I've got the little one.' Then it sniggered and looked at Samhorse. 'You've got the big one.'

'Then I must be Georgehorse,' said the third horse looking up and staring at George. 'I don't feel like running just now, so if you don't mind, we'll have a rest and go later.' It nodded as if there could not be any argument on the subject.

'You are one lazy horse,' said Scorpio, moving to stand in front of the little horse and staring into its eyes. 'I don't want any trouble with you,' he tapped him gently on the nose with his finger. 'We are going now and we will all be running.'

Georgehorse started to complain, but the hunchback cut him short with a threat. 'You'll be pegged out with me if we get caught, so you'll run as fast as you can.'

There was no question about whether the friends could ride a horse. Scorpio simply assumed that everybody could ride, so he handed each of them a saddle to put onto the backs of their horses.

'That is the wrong way round!' snorted Georgehorse.

'Beg your pardon,' said George, turning the saddle the other way.

'Do you mind?' said Samhorse turning his head and nudging at Sam. 'That is too tight.'

'Excuse me,' said Sam and he loosened the strap that he had just fastened under the horse's belly.

Once saddled, Millyhorse walked to a stool and suggested to Milly that it would help her climb onto his back. This she did gingerly and, although she felt very nervous at being so high in the air, she was excited at the prospect of riding a horse for the first time.

Realising that his new friends were not used to riding, Scorpio spoke to the horses. 'Follow me, we will walk first, then we will trot and we only gallop when I say so.'

With an unexpected agility, Scorpio leapt up onto his own mount, a ragged looking animal but with a sharp gleam in its eyes, and lead the way out of the stable. The three friends followed dutifully, though really it was the horses who did the following - all they had to do was hold on tight. In a line they left the inn and set off across country away from the river.

Drago, who had been lying in the sun outside, keeping his peace, had kept a keen eye on the unfolding events. As the horses trotted by, he slowly raised himself, shook the dust from his fur, and obediently trotted along behind without saying a word.

Soon they came to a large signpost where a road split into four directions.

'This is the crossroads. From here you can get everywhere,' said Scorpio, by way of explanation.

They all looked up at it. The four directions were marked DOME CITY, NOGOODLANDS, LITTLEWICH and THE SEA OF ISLANDS.

They all turned to Scorpio for an explanation, but he simply said, 'I can't read the sign, but I do know the way.' And with a nudge to the flank of his horse it broke into a trot and took the road that lead to the city. The other horses followed suit and the friends were too busy trying to stay upright on their saddles to worry about anything else.

Once they got used to the trotting of the horses, they surveyed the surrounding area. The road wound ahead, following the river as it snaked through the countryside. On the far side of the river were lush fields and neatly trimmed hedgerows, but on this side loomed a dense forest full of tall pines and tangled brambles.

'You know,' said George looking up at the sky. 'This is very strange. The sun is warm, I have never seen a cloud in the sky and the temperature never changes. It is always warm and pleasant.'

'I rather like it,' replied Sam, unconcerned by the curious nature of the climate.

Drago stopped all the talking by barking loudly to get their attention. His voice was dry and rasping. 'I think we may have company,' he called out.

All the horses stopped of their own accord and turned to look behind them. Milly and Sam were caught off balance and both fell forwards onto the neck of their horses and, although Milly regained her balance, Sam slid out of his saddle and fell to the ground.

Further back down the road they could clearly see a dust cloud raised by the horses pulling the Robes carts.

'Yikes,' screeched Scorpio. 'It's them! It's the Robes! We must escape. Come on horses, follow me!'

The horses needed no encouragement, and they certainly didn't need steering. All they wanted was to run like the wind. As soon as the hunchback and Scorpiohorse set off at high speed, the others followed instantly.

George was expecting it and leant forward to keep himself low in the saddle. Soon the wind was whipping through his hair. Milly also leaned forward and to keep her balance, wrapping both arms tightly around the neck of Millyhorse, whose hooves scratched the ground frantically as he sought to keep up with the horse in front.

Samhorse was right behind, but without Sam, who was still sitting on the road further back. Although he shouted loudly after them, nobody heard a word. He had to watch his friends and their horses disappearing at high speed around the next bend.

As he stood up, brushing the dust from his clothes, he heard the sound of approaching hooves. There was only one thing for him to do - turn and run!

It was only when Samhorse overtook Milly that she realised Sam was missing. 'Stop!' she screeched to the others. 'We've left Sam behind!'

'No, don't stop!' Sam's voice came from the other side of her. 'Keep going!'

Turning her head, she gasped at the startling sight of Sam, running alongside and keeping pace with the horses. George and Scorpio turned to look as well. Sam's arms were pumping up and down, his head was thrown back as he sucked air into his lungs and his legs were pounding along the road in a blur.

'I was changed after all,' he shouted out. 'This is magnificent. Keep going all of you or I'll leave you behind!'

The group raced on as hard as they could, trying

to put some distance between themselves and their pursuers. Finally, Scorpio brought them up to a slow trot and turned round in the saddle to look back along the road. The dust cloud showed him the Robes were getting closer, despite their best efforts.

'We have to leave the road,' the hunchback said in a tired voice. 'The horses can't run forever. Maybe we can hide in the forest.'

Sam was bent double and gasping for air as his body struggled to come to terms with the effort of running so fast.

George glanced back down the road.

'If the Robes are using the same sort of chariot we saw in Littlewich and the same sort of magneto road to draw the power they need to keep going, then they have to stay on the road.'

'I have never been in the forest before,' said Scorpio, looking up at the tall, dark trees swaying overhead. 'It's very dangerous, nobody ever goes there.' He bit his lip and let out a long, exhausted sigh.

'We have no choice,' Milly said. 'If we take the horses and hide close to the road then maybe the Robes will give up looking and go away.'

Dismounting they stood in a group, each one was carrying the small bag of provisions that Scorpio had hastily put together for them back at the inn.

A shout went up from behind them and on looking back they realised that the chariots were only seconds away, so without any further discussion, they rushed into the woods.

But the horses had their own plans and stayed firmly on the road.

Scorpio tried to persuade them to hide as well. 'Come on horses, the Robes will peg you out,' he called to them.

Georgehorse reared in the air and waved his hooves defiantly. 'Not likely,' he said. 'We'll say you forced us into it.'

Scorpio growled at the pompous animal.

'And anyway,' continued the horse, 'I'd rather face the Robes than get eaten by the monsters in there.'

'Well go on then!' cried Scorpio. 'But make sure you go back to the inn, or I'll turn you into stew!'

'I don't think so,' sniffed the horse, and trotted off the way it had come.

The other two followed, but Scorpiohorse waited, uncertain and unwilling to leave so easily.

'You go too,' said Scorpio, with a gentle nod. 'And see they go home like I told them.'

With a nod, the horse turned and followed the other three back towards the inn.

As it went, Scorpio saw that the Robes had only one more corner to turn and they would be upon them.

'We must move. Fast!'

9

THE TANGLED WOOD

George led the way round big tree trunks that towered upwards to a green canopy above. As they walked deeper into the forest, the canopy grew thicker and the light faded, the high trees blocking out the sun. The air became cold and still. Milly shivered.

'I don't think we need to go too far in,' she said nervously.

'I agree,' said Drago, his eyes darting from left to right as he tried to keep a look out in all directions at once. 'We've no idea what could be lurking.'

There was no path, just tall trees, tangled bushes and dead leaves covering the ground. It was very quiet, only the sound of their own feet crunching the undergrowth followed their every step.

A great screech stopped them in their tracks. It came from the trees above. Looking up they saw several monkey-like creatures scampering along the lower branches. One by one the creatures stopped moving and sat down to observe the newcomers. Each one had a small head with sharp pointed ears and large staring eyes that never blinked. White whiskers on their chins made them look quite cute, until they opened their wide mouths to reveal blood red teeth shaped like miniature daggers.

Another screech came from behind the friends and made them jump. Whirling around, they saw that more of the creatures were sitting along the lower branches of the trees behind them.

'We're surrounded,' hissed George, in a tense whisper.

Nervously the friends backed up together into a small circle. With a loud yelp, one of the monkeys jumped to the ground. It landed on short skinny legs and balanced on a long tail as it strutted towards them. Although it only came up to Milly's waist, its fierce look and swaggering walk made her tremble. Getting closer, it hissed and stared at her.

'Stand back!' she said, summoning up the firmest voice she could manage and waving her hands at the creature.

Three more of the monkeys jumped to the ground and sloped towards them. Drago growled; Milly was being threatened and that made his hairs twitch. He moved forward and placed himself in front of her. His neck was a mass of pointed bristles and his body began to grow, thick muscles rippling down his legs and across his back. In less than a minute, Drago was ready to fight. He snarled and showed the creature his own set of razor-like fangs.

Milly clenched her fists.

All four of the monkeys darted at them at once. Drago snapped sideways at the biggest of them, catching it on the arm. The next one moved rapidly to Milly who drew back her fist and punched it on its white whiskered chin.

Whirling around, Drago intercepted a third

attacker. One fast bite was enough to send it away
screeching in pain. Before Milly could defend
herself again, the next monkey snatched her bag
from her shoulder and raced off with it into the forest.
Without hesitating, Sam leapt after it, moving at a

tremendous speed. He caught up with the creature just as it started to climb a tree. Wrapping his arms around its waist, he pulled it back to the ground and snatched the bag from its grasp. The lightning speed with which he returned to his friends startled the other monkeys in the trees, who had begun to jump to the ground to join in the attack.

Milly dealt with several more of the creatures, and each one staggered back before crashing in a heap. Drago leapt every way he could, snapping and snarling at every beast that came near. The noise became deafening as the creatures screeched endlessly. Although quite small in comparison, Scorpio had powerful arms and managed to defend himself well against any monkey who tried to take his bag.

But the monkeys kept coming, and George, struggling in the midst of chaos, could see they would soon be over-run if they couldn't get away. He was looking in vain for a way out when, quite suddenly, the creatures began to back away, screeching and waving their tails. One by one they climbed back into the trees and took their places once again on the branches. Many of them sat licking wounds or rubbing bruised chins.

Seeing they had made their retreat, Drago walked slowly round the little group, teeth bared, eyes glaring, sending a clear message to any monkey who might think to resume the attack.

Gradually, the monkeys melted back into the forest from whence they'd come. The friends stood still, gasping for breath, and listening to the silence that now enveloped them.

'That was pretty close,' said George, dusting off his jacket and straightening his cap.

'If we hadn't been changed,' said Sam, wiping his brow with a rag from his pocket, 'we'd be shredded by now.' He smiled and even gave a small, but exhausted, laugh. Looking at Milly, he added, 'You were magnificent! What a shock those beasts got. That'll teach them to pick on the smallest.'

They all laughed, glad the fight was over and none of them had been hurt.

'We'd best get moving,' said George. 'Last thing we want is them coming back again!'

As they walked on, climbing over the mass of spiked brambles, a weak beam of light found its way through the canopy of trees and shone down on the group. Scorpio shaded his eyes as he looked upwards.

'It'll be dark soon and we will have to spend the night in the forest,' he said quietly and glanced around with a worried look on his face.

'We could head back to the road,' suggested Sam. 'The Robes may have gone by now.'

'I'm sure they will,' agreed Scorpio, frowning at Sam, 'but who wants to be out in the open at dusk. Are you forgetting the Muttons?'

'Then we have to find somewhere safe to spend the night,' said George, studying the terrain around them.

'How about up a tree?' was Sam's next suggestion.

Milly gasped. 'But what about those monkey creatures? They climb trees!'

'Monkeys that roam about during the day must sleep at night,' said Drago thoughtfully. The others murmured a hopeful agreement.

'It's probably the best option we have,' said George. 'I can't imagine what sort of wild animals roam around at night. At least the monkeys know we can fight back.'

A blood curdling howl, somewhere away in the distance, split the silence around them. A prolonged roar that sounded very much like a lion looking for its dinner immediately answered it.

'A tree, definitely a tree,' said Sam, and he led the way forward looking all around for a suitable one to climb.

An anxious time was spent searching for the right spot as the light faded to an unsettling gloom. A growing chorus of strange calls and grunts signalled the waking of the forest nightlife. One huge tree trunk loomed up in front of them like a giant with its arms outstretched. Scorpio looked up at the branches and nodded approvingly. 'This looks suitable,' he said. 'It's big and we could climb quite high.'

'I'll check it out,' volunteered Sam, who bent down, took a deep breath and leaped a good ten feet to take a firm grip on one of the lowest branches. With a few more agile lunges, he had climbed up much further and disappeared from view.

Five minutes later, a rustling of the leaves

announced his return. He dropped out of the tree and landed beside them, smirking happily.

'It's perfect,' he said, with great excitement. 'I went right to the top. It's pretty much the tallest tree in the forest. I could see for miles. The city is that way.' He pointed to show them. 'And the river flows around the forest in a huge circle.' Again he waved an arm to show them what he meant. 'But best of all, there's a hollow in the tree about half way up that will be perfect for us to spend the night in.'

'I'm not good with trees,' said Drago, looking at the swaying branches above his head. The others followed his gaze and a tense silence descended as they tried to find a solution to the problem.

'Don't worry about me,' said the dog bravely. 'I'll be fine. I'll hide in a bush or something.'

'No you won't,' said Milly, throwing her arms around his neck and pulling him close. 'I want you right next to me.'

'Once we get him onto that first branch, it should be easy,' said Sam. 'The branches are all close together and we can push and pull him as far as the hollow.'

'I know,' said Milly, 'if George can bend forward and stand firm, then Drago can run up and jump on him. If he puts his paws onto George's shoulders and leaps for the first branch, Sam can sit on the branch and help to pull him up.'

Milly's suggestion was tried and, after a few goes, it worked. Using George's back for support, Drago leapt high enough for Sam to catch him and help him scramble onto the first branch. Milly and Scorpio cheered as Drago reached it, but George roared with pain as the dog's back feet scrabbled about his ears and tangled in his hair.

Once the dog was up, George brushed himself off, rubbed his sore ears then replaced his cap firmly on his head. 'That's the last time I let a dog use me as a springboard!' he muttered. He then helped Milly and Scorpio into the tree before joining them on the first branch.

With Sam leading the way, they climbed high enough to reach the hollow in the mighty trunk, leaving the tops of other trees some way down below them.

Once settled inside the hollow tree, they opened the bags that Scorpio had given them. Hungrily they tucked in to the food, mostly bread and chicken and an apple each, savouring every morsel. It wasn't much, but it tasted good nonetheless.

'Do you think anyone lives here?' asked Scorpio at last, in a hushed voice. 'I mean, it's such a handy little place, some sort of creature must use it as home.'

This thought had not occurred to any of them before. Nervously, they all looked around to see if there was any sign of an existing occupant who might turn up at any moment.

'There are a lot of small twigs and a few feathers,' said George, 'which would indicate a bird of some sort.'

'Birds are all right,' said Milly hopefully. 'Aren't

they?'

George frowned. 'You never know in this place. I bet they're not all like Batty...'

Sam pulled out his pocket knife. 'Let's cut some branches off, sharpen the tips and then we have some spears. It might help. Anyway, it pays to be prepared.' They managed to get three pointed sticks together before they settled down to finish their meagre rations, and again they sat facing the entrance.

Suddenly a blast of air blew into the hollow tree, accompanied by a great flapping noise. The weak daylight that remained cast a shadow into the tree as the claws of a huge bird grasped the branch outside the opening. They froze in shock and the boys clutched their spears tightly. A very large bird had settled down on the branch and now popped its head into the hideout.

'Oh dear,' said Drago. 'This doesn't look good.'

It was the head of a very large eagle, with bright, black eyes and a curved, yellow beak. Short white feathers covered the head and neck with long, brown feathers covering the shoulders and wings. Nobody spoke, they just sat there petrified. Moving the head in a slow circle the bird scrutinised them one at a time. Finally its gaze settled on Scorpio and the head cocked itself sideways and the eyes blinked slowly.

Slowly, the little hunchback reached into his bag and pulled out a piece of bread. He stood up and moved towards the big bird and, holding out his hand, offered it the food. Delicately, the sharp beak took it and, in a quick gulp, it was swallowed.

The staring eyes transferred their gaze to Sam, who received a nudge from Scorpio. Silently, Sam fished out a piece of chicken and held it out towards the bird. Again the beak pecked it neatly out of his hand. Then it was George's turn. Without daring to break the silence and holding his breath, he offered the bird another piece of bread. It was accepted and Milly then followed suit with her last strip of meat.

The eagle removed its head from the hollow in the tree and, to everyone's surprise, Scorpio joined the bird just outside the entrance. The friends watched as the young boy smiled, tickled the eagle under the chin and stroked the feathers on the top

of his head. After a while the bird hunched down, fluffed its feathers and settled down using the branch as a perch for the night. The entrance was now effectively blocked and Scorpio returned.

As he settled back down, he whispered to the others. 'Lovely bird, that. Don't you think?'

All eyes stared at him in surprise.

IN THE HEART OF THE CITY

Having kept a safe watch over them for the rest of the night, the giant eagle departed from her perch as soon as dawn broke. In spite of her protection, it had been an uncomfortable night for them.

'Feathers and twigs may be fine for a bird,' grumbled Sam, as the small party threaded its way down to the base of the tree, 'but I'd rather a mattress any day. Even one of the hard ones back at the hall!'

'Stop grumbling!' said George, also feeling stiff in every joint. 'At least we were safe, and that counts for a lot round here.'

When they had all reached the forest floor, and given themselves a good stretch, George led the way back to the edge of the forest. Stepping out of the forbidding trees, they found themselves once more bathed in bright sunlight. It felt good on their weary backs, and they moved on with a brighter step, cutting across a meadow to link up with the river they had seen flowing into the city. A narrow path ran alongside the river bank broken and rutted in places, but otherwise fairly passable. They trudged along it in silence for a while, each contending with the growing feeling of hunger in their bellies. The nearer they got to the city, the more signs of life appeared around them, with boats chugging up and down and carts and horses travelling along the far bank.

They tried to walk in as casual a fashion as they could, but it was not easy; three human children, a dog and a hunchback were bound to attract attention. As they walked on, they could feel eyes beginning to track their every move.

The river wound round the base of a large hill. Sam suggested they climb the hill and survey the lie of the land. After a brief but wearisome climb, made worse by the lack of food, they lay down side by side at the summit, gazing down at the Dome City spread out before them.

The city was similar to Littlewich, only far larger. There were red roofed houses of all shapes and sizes with roads and alleyways cutting through them in every direction. It was dominated by a huge domed building in the centre, where the river split into two to surround it and made it look like a castle of some sort, surrounded by a deep moat.

'It's a very strange land we've found,' said George. 'It rather looks like a medieval town that has been stuck in a time warp for hundreds of years.'

'Apart from the carts with no wheels!' added Sam. 'That's more like the future! I wish I knew how they worked...'

'And look at that dome,' said Milly. She was lying on her stomach staring intently at the white building in the centre. As well as the river, it appeared to be surrounded by long, low, wooden sheds attached to one side of it, as though added on as an afterthought. From the top of the dome there rose a shimmering column of vapour, stretching high into the sky and spreading out far above the clouds. Milly pointed this out, fascinated by its mysterious, ethereal glow.

'I'll bet it's the source of the energy that powers the city and everything else. These people have got bright lights and magneto roads, and boats that don't need rowing or sails. There must be something that makes it all work, something that isn't coal or gas...'

'Well,' said Sam, following her train of thought,

'if that's the engine room, then I'd say that's where Tom will be. What do you think Scorpio?'

'I have never travelled this far from the inn before. But you are probably right. Clever children are brought to work in the engine room and it's supposed to be an amazing place.'

'What now then?' asked Milly.

There was silence as each one tried to think of a plan.

'If Tom is in that dome place then we need to rescue him,' George said slowly. 'To do that we will probably need another boat.' Turning to Milly, he added, 'Can Tom swim?'

'I don't think so,' she frowned and tried to remember.

'That river is not safe,' said Sam warily. 'We have met sharks in it, one-eyed fish and crocodiles! Who ever heard of sharks in a river? What other surprises does it hold?'

The others all shrugged.

'Changed or not,' he went on. 'I have no intention of going in that water ever again.'

'Then we have to find a boat,' said Milly emphatically.

'Not necessarily,' said George. 'I can swim and breathe under water and I'm the only one who could cross over to the dome without being seen. I propose that I swim across and explore. If I find Tom, then I can come back and we try and find a boat. At night-time we can sneak across again, under cover of darkness, and rescue him.'

The others agreed, so they returned to the river bank and started to walk towards the city outskirts.

'We must avoid a meeting with the Robes at all costs,' said Drago. 'Let me walk ahead with Scorpio and scout around a bit. If we see any Robes coming, I'll bark twice to warn you.'

'Good idea,' said George. 'Let's do that.'

So Scorpio and Drago set off in front of the others. It was just as well, because as soon as they reached the streets of the city, Drago barked twice in quick succession. They happened to be passing a baker's shop at the time, so they opened the door and darted inside. It seemed a good place to hide, indeed it was the only place to hide, because a few moments later three Robes came past and actually stopped to look in at the shop window. The fugitives held their breath. Fortunately for them, the Robes were more interested in the goods for sale and didn't notice anyone inside.

Turning their backs on the window, the children chose bread, cakes and drinks from the shopkeeper and, against the wishes of their rumbling tummies, took as long as they could in buying them. Luckily, Sam had enough leather strips left for the purchase. Out of the corners of their eyes, they watched the Robes' movements, in case they had to make a quick getaway. But the Robes had their copious hoods draped over their heads and what could be seen of their unsmiling faces seemed interested only in the available produce.

Finally, the Robes moved on without buying

anything. A short while later, the three children left the shop, hungrily munching on their rolls and cakes, and their knapsacks full with more provisions. Scorpio and Drago were waiting for them some way along the street. Milly and Sam handed out some food to them while George kept an eye out.

'It's very quiet today,' he said at last, 'which is good for us.'

It was the middle of the afternoon when they came to the moat surrounding the dome. They found a narrow log to sit on from where they could study the dome and the sheds surrounding it. The occasional Minling passed by and gave them a sideways glance, but nobody stopped to say anything, which was just as well.

All around them they could hear the constant hum of activity coming from the dome, and they watched in awe the great plume of shimmering mist as it rose upwards and into the clouds above. Among the sheds, people would come and go, sometimes alone or in pairs or groups. From this distance it was hard to tell if they were Minlings or real children. What was not hard to see was that wherever they went, there was always a Robe never very far behind.

Shadows lengthened as the afternoon wore on and George, feeling restless, stepped forward to survey the water beneath them. Unlike the river it looked still, almost lifeless, but he could see it was clean enough to swim in.

'Now is a good time,' he announced, returning

to the group, and checking to see if anyone was watching.

Taking his clothes off for a late afternoon swim might have seemed a perfectly normal thing to do at home, but here it could well have drawn unwelcome attention. Instead, he quietly walked back down to the side of the moat and, after another quick look around, slid into the water fully clothed and disappeared from sight.

Anxiously, the others looked hard at the surface of the moat across to where the dome loomed high on the other side. They could not see any crocodiles or the tell tail fins of sharks lurking around, but Milly did spot something else moving through the murky depths.

'Look,' she cried, pointing at the water. 'Eye fish!'

Sure enough they saw the tiny creatures gathering at the point where George had entered the water. They appeared quite calm to begin with, but then, in a sudden flurry of flapping tails, the eye fish dived below the surface and swam away. Following their line, Milly saw the triangular fin of a shark moving steadily across the surface. She screamed in shock, clasping her hand to her mouth. There was nothing they could do except watch in horror as the shark swerved, circled and then, flapping its tail with a great swish, dived down deep and out of sight.

George soon got used to breathing underwater

again. In fact, he felt it to be almost second nature this time around. Staying close to the bottom of the moat, he swam slowly towards the other side of the island on which the Dome was built. It was quiet under the water but for the sound of his blood pumping furiously in his ears. As his eyes got used to the subdued light, he could clearly see the route he ought to take. Unlike the muddy bank where he had first waded in, the far side of the moat was solid rock, with some stone and brick construction built into it. Two little eye fish overtook him and he slowed down to avoid swimming into them. They looked like overgrown tadpoles with their stubby tails, huge eyes and long, pointed snouts.

As he watched them, more came to join him and in a second there was a great flurry of eye fish all about him. At that moment the shark appeared. George felt his heart leap. He stopped swimming altogether and let his feet drift down to the very bottom of the moat. His heart pounding, the throbbing in his ears even louder than before, he stood, terrified.

Looking around, it was hard to see which way to move in order to escape from the shark. Rather than have the creature grab him from behind as he tried to swim away, he decided to stay and fight. The only weapon he had was a pocket knife, useless against a great shark, but he decided to get it out anyway. As he struggled to remove it from his pocket, he noticed that more and more of the eye fish were gathering in front of him. Soon there were so many of them that he almost lost sight of the shark. He tried in vain to sweep them away, to clear his vision, but they just kept crowding in on him, enveloping him in their fluttering, flickering fins. For a moment he thought it had turned away, but then he caught site of the white belly and gleaming teeth as it sped towards him, launching its attack.

As one, the shoal of eye fish darted towards the shark in retaliation. Immediately, George found a

wall of the little fish between him and the attacking beast. Confused, the shark turned away and swam in a great circle, as though to reassess the nature of its prey. George swivelled as well, watching the beast as it turned again and thrust itself forward in a second attack. Without hesitation, the swarm of eye fish rushed past George with their tails flapping frantically and in one great mass they swam right at the shark as they had before. Again the beast turned away and the eye fish swirled round and returned to surround George.

Three more times the shark tried to reach him but each time it was frightened away by the eye fish. Finally, the great beast gave up the fight and, turning tail, swam away into the darkness. Once the shark had gone, most of the little eye fish dispersed as well and soon George was left to swim slowly across to the island. Like an escort, posted on sentry duty, a few of the little eye fish swam alongside him until they were sure he was out of danger and able to make it back onto dry land.

He had started to haul himself up the rocky edge when he noticed a small boat chugging along above him. Instinctively, he followed it and, when it pulled up onto a small slipway, George allowed his head to break the surface of the water so he could watched the boat land.

The slipway ran alongside a couple of the long, low sheds that surrounded the dome. Two Robes were pulling the boat a little way out of the water and securing it to an iron ring embedded in the ground.

One of the Robes was considerably larger than the other and walked with a slight limp. Together they headed towards a door in the side of the building where the smaller one stooped down as if to retrieve something. George inched in closer to the edge and raised himself slightly to get a better view. He saw the smaller Robe reach under the wooden joist of the shed and pull out a rusty looking key. After unlocking the door, both Robes disappeared inside, slamming the door shut behind them.

George pulled himself out of the water and waited for a few moments before creeping towards the door. Listening for any sounds inside, he heard none and so, gripping the door handle, he gave it a turn. To his relief the door had not been locked again. With a final check behind him, he pulled open the door and slipped inside.

He found himself in a long room that appeared to be a dormitory. Beds were lined up against the walls on either side of the room and beside each one stood a small cupboard. It reminded George, in every way, of his own dormitory back at Mercy Hall. Even the air had the same dusty, stale smell to it. He shook himself, trying to get the memory out of his head, and steeled himself to continue his investigations.

The only other door in the room was at the far end. George presumed it led into the dome itself and, because the dormitory was empty, he guessed that the two Robes he'd seen earlier must have passed through it.

To the side of the room several white coats were hanging on pegs. In order to cover his wet clothes, George took one and put it on. It fitted him surprisingly well. Moving over to the door, he opened it slightly and peeped out. On the other side he saw a corridor leading to some stairs. Taking a deep breath, he ventured out of the room and, as quietly as he could, tip-toed up the stairs. Reaching the top of them, he found another door which led into a corridor, only this time there were windows overlooking the inside of the dome. The air in the corridor was very warm, almost stifling. Putting out his hand to touch a window, he could feel the

increase in temperature through the glass.

In the heart of the dome some figures moved about the floor in an apparently aimless fashion. Each of them held a clipboard as they moved about, looking at the dials and little windows that covered a great steel structure in the centre of the room, shaped like a large doughnut. Above the doughnut, a heat haze shimmered all the way to the roof of the dome and out through a large circular opening in the roof.

'This must be the power generation room,' thought George, studiously examining the doughnut, 'and that must be some sort of energy generator.'

Remembering he had to look for Tom and stay out of sight, he moved silently down the corridor where he found that the doors down one side of the room had little windows in them. With every step he took his heart beat faster and louder. He anticipated being discovered at any moment. His whole body was poised to flee, back to the stairs and out, into the safety of the lake, where he knew he could swim away and no-one would even think of following him.

At the third door, he peeped through the little window. The two Robes he saw in the boat were standing opposite each other across a metal table of some sort, with drawers down one side. The smaller of the two had seated himself on a stool and was taking a leather bag out of one of the drawers. As he did so, the larger one flipped back the hood of his gown and shook his big, beetroot head. George got the shock of his life.

The limping figure he'd seen earlier should have triggered some memory, but the stark truth hit him like a thump in the chest, and fairly took the wind from his sails. There before him, on the other side of the door, stood Jethro Barking, the headmaster of the Mercy Hall Orphanage. Under the orange gown he wore the same pin-striped suit, with it's greasy sheen and frayed edges.

George was so shocked he could hardly breathe. How could Barking be here? And talking with a Robe?

As he watched, the Robe handed the small, leather pouch to Barking who, opening it up, peered inside and gave a big, leering grin. He then turned his eyes to the door.

George ducked out of sight. Why had Barking looked? Had George been seen?

He stood with his back to the wall, breathing heavily. A growing panic threatened to overwhelm him. He felt confused, with no idea what to do. His first instinct was to run, as fast as he could, to get back and tell his friends. But he knew he had to find Tom. Milly expected it of him. He couldn't go back without, at the very least, some trace of his existence.

Steeling himself, he took another glance through the window into the room. Neither of the men were looking towards the door, so at least he could be sure they had not seen him. Both were sitting down now, chatting with each other and shaking hands. George tried to make out some words, but the doors were so thick, all he could hear was muffled conversation.

He ducked away and out of sight, his mind racing. What was Old Barking Mad doing here? What was in the bag he'd been given? Did he know about Tom and the other children? He must do! He couldn't be here and not know, which meant... He'd arranged the kidnaps!

Again, George felt a terrible urge to run and get away from the place as soon as he could. Forcing himself to relax and think clearly, he came up with a plan.

'If Tom is being held prisoner here, along with other people,' he told himself, 'then the dormitory is probably where they spend the night. If I go back there and find a way to leave a message for Tom, then I can tell him about Milly and our plan.'

Risking another glance into the room, he saw the two men stand and, with another handshake, turn towards the door.

George fled. He reached the dormitory without being seen and quickly went from bed to bed, rummaging through the bedside cupboards. Half way along, he found one with a bag inside and the name TOM BANKS scrawled on it in black ink. Inside the bag he found a pencil and a few scraps of paper. Quickly he wrote a message:

Milly sent me. If you want to leave this place, wave a light in the window three times tonight after dark and wait. We will bring a boat to you before dawn.

Leaving the paper on his bedside cupboard where he must surely see it, George prayed that if someone else did find it, then it would be a friend of Tom's and he would get it anyway.

There was no time to waste. He could hear footsteps approaching the inner door. George headed for the exit at the far end of the dormitory, leaving it unlocked so as not to arouse suspicions. He crept quietly past the little boat drawn up on the quay. Although tempted to take it, he knew it would soon be missed and the alarm would be raised. Climbing back down the rocks, he slid into the moat and looked anxiously all around for the shark. It was not in sight, but some little eye fish appeared, perhaps they had even been waiting for him, and he welcomed them with a smile. It seemed like they were there to watch out for him again on his journey back across the water. If they were, he was not about to refuse their help.

Once underwater, he immediately felt strong and full of energy. It was a power he enjoyed and, with the eye fish darting all around him, he decided to see how fast he could swim. When he reached the bottom of the lake, he tensed his muscles and set off using a powerful breaststroke. He was amazed at the speed he could go and, in only a few strokes, noticed he had left the eye fish far behind. He stopped and, once they caught up with him, set out again at a slower speed, allowing them to swim alongside him. He might be fast in the water, but he was still aware the shark must be lurking somewhere, and the shark was fast too.

As he approached the side of the bank where he'd left Milly and Sam, he popped his head out of the water to check that he was going in the right direction. He saw them all right.

Just at that moment, as they sat on the log, with Drago sleeping on the ground beside them, four Robes jumped them from behind. Two burly Robes grabbed Milly and pinned her arms to her side. The other two had Sam flat on the ground and were busy trying to secure his legs. Scorpio had moved very quickly and escaped. He was now standing to one side and jumping up and down in a very agitated fashion. The attack had been so sudden, Drago was only just waking to the commotion around him.

Ducking down into the water again, George swam very fast towards them and came leaping out onto the bank. He roared as he ran up the slope and threw himself towards the log in the hope of surprising the attackers.

The suddenness of George's appearance, and his brave attack, worked. The Robes loosened their grip on Milly in order to face him. It was all Milly needed. She was already angry and managed to get one arm free. The power surged within her and she punched one of the Robes hard on the jaw. The effect was startling. Her attacker dropped like a stone and the other Robe made the mistake of letting go of Milly completely. Clenching her fist and swinging her arm around, she punched the second Robe full in the chest with her elbow. He gave a pained cry and, gasping for breath, fell flat on his back.

The two Robes holding Sam released him and took a step away from the awesome Milly. At that moment, a crowd of Robes came rushing and shouting from over the hill, some of them waving sticks. When the friends looked up and saw them, they instinctively decided to run, rather than face overwhelming odds. Scorpio darted in to release Drago, who had by now grown in size and was jumping around in a fury, the log trailing after him, hampering his movement.

'Settle down, big dog,' he said in a calming voice that seemed to do the trick. 'Let me help you.'

Drago stood still for a moment, giving Scorpio time to untie the bench and get him free.

As the group turned to flee, Sam, fearing that Milly would be too slow, scooped her up in his arms and raced on ahead.

George glanced at Scorpio and realised that his ungainly limp would prevent him from escaping at all. He grabbed him by the arm and told him to climb on his back. But instead of running, George waded back into the water and started swimming at high speed, following Sam who was speeding along the path beside the river. Drago ran easily alongside him and barked his encouragement to them all.

The river led them away from the city and back

out into the wild lands. Soon, the pursuers had been left a long way behind and appeared to have given up the chase. Sam came to a stop and gasped for breath as he let Milly slide to the ground.

'I do like this power,' he shouted to George, who was crawling out of the river with a very sodden Scorpio on his back.

They all laughed and, seeing no Robes coming after them, took shelter in some bushes to catch their breath.

'Prepare yourselves for a shock,' said George, once they had revived a little. 'You'll never guess who I saw in the Dome?'

'Who?' asked Milly, hoping it might have been her long lost brother.

'Old Barking Mad himself!' said George, eyes wide.

'Never!' they both gasped in astonishment.

'What was he doing there?' asked Sam. 'I can't believe it!'

'He was there all right, in a boat wearing an orange gown, and I followed him into the dome. While looking for Tom, I spotted him in a room with a Robe, smirking and gloating over a leather bag.'

'What was in it?' asked Milly.

'I don't know. I couldn't quite see, but Barking looked very pleased with himself. I wanted to get a look, but I thought finding Tom was more urgent.'

He then told them about the message he'd left in the dormitory and they realised they had to get back to the dome in time to see the signal, and with a boat big enough to rescue all the prisoners.

It was late in the afternoon. Sam looked anxiously at the sky.

'It'll be dark before long. How do we find a boat and still avoid the Robes?' He looked anxiously behind them along the path, 'I don't think they'll give up that easily. They must be planning something.'

Out in the river several boats were in view. Scorpio noticed a large barge, some distance away, similar to the ones that brought cargo to the quay in Littlewich. 'That power you have,' he said, turning to George, 'swimming like a fish, it's amazing. Perhaps you could follow that boat until it docks, then when it does maybe you could borrow it and return to find us.'

'That would give us a boat, and we could hide in the middle of the river! The Robes would never think of looking there for us,' said Milly in delight. 'What a good idea!'

They all stared at the distant barge. Two distinctive orange coloured figures showed that Robes were at the helm.

'Leave it to me,' said George, and, once again, he slid into the water and disappeared from sight.

The barge floated sedately back up the river towards the city. It came alongside the Dome and, just as the light faded, pulled into a dock by a warehouse. The two Robes disembarked and tied it up to an iron ring in the side of the quay. Chatting together in hushed tones, the Robes walked away without a backward glance. As soon as they were out of sight, a hand came out of the water and undid the rope. The boat floated gently away from the quay and soon reached the middle of the river. To a casual observer, nobody appeared to be on board, yet the boat moved steadily along with the current, leaving a gentle wake behind it.

Beneath the surface, George, the rope tied around his middle, was pulling it along with his powerful breaststroke. When he felt he was far enough away from the dock, he climbed out of the water and into the boat. Starting up the engine, he took the borrowed boat back upriver towards the spot where his friends were waiting.

It was getting late and, as he passed the Dome, he saw a curtain move in the dormitory window. Three times it moved and each time a bright light escaped. George was in no doubt - it was the signal!

'Right,' he said to himself, with a feeling of mounting excitement, 'now the fun really starts!'

II

ESCAPE FROM THE CITY

Tom was exhausted.

As he trudged back to the dormitory with all the other children, he reflected on the hard day he'd had in the Engine Room. Operating the machines that kept the city running day and night was a gruelling task. He understood little of how they worked or what they did. All he knew was how to follow instructions, press the right buttons at the right time, pull the right levers... This was what he did, day in, day out.

But today had been different. Earlier, standing up on the balcony that ran around the interior of the Dome, he'd seen the man whom he'd always suspected of selling him into this slavery - Jethro Barking, the person he hated most in the world.

When their eyes had met, for a brief moment, his former headmaster had sneered, then turned away. There was nothing Tom could do. To shout or protest was to invite punishment from the Robes who watched over the workers at all times, and their punishment was always harsh.

Arriving back in the dormitory, he was about to slump on his bed when the day had changed again, in a very unexpected way. Lying on his bedside cupboard he found a slip of paper neatly folded and with his name written on it. Taking it, he unfolded the paper and began to read.

'Unbelievable!' he gasped. Those who shared the dormitory with him heard his astonished exclamation and came over to see what he was reading. Tom read the message out loud to them all. The atmosphere in the room changed immediately from worn out despondency to one of feverish excitement. The nine scruffy urchins with him were now full of hope at the prospect of an escape, of a chance at freedom...

Tom quickly took control of the moment. At fourteen years old he was growing into a strong and resourceful young man. His brown eyes sparkled, just like Milly's did when she was excited. He held up both hands to stop the sudden outburst of loud chattering.

'Quiet,' he hissed. 'We must not do anything out of the ordinary. We do not want to attract attention.'

His friend Ralph took the paper out of his hand and stared at it. The news was too good to be true and he just had to read it for himself. Ralph was the same age as Tom. The two of them had been captured around the same time on the road out of the orphanage. He was tall, slim and always cheerful, despite suffering the same deprivations as the rest of them. Giving a silent yippee he jumped up and down with excitement.

'I hope the Robes don't call for me tonight,' said Singer Smith anxiously. She was a girl of about fourteen years old, who had a beautiful voice and very often the Robes in the engine room would make her sing for them in the evening. They all fell silent for a moment and, squeezing their eyes tight shut, dared to hope that nothing would happen to prevent them from escaping that night.

Tom looked around the group and realised how much he liked each of them. As well as Ralph and Singer, there were the young twins, Raffer and Agnes, always up to mischief and who frequently got them all into trouble. Their best friend and accomplice was Charlie Trinder, a boy of the same age who had lived rough on the streets of London. Robert Williams, the oldest of the group at seventeen, already had the mind of a brilliant scientist. Billy and Daisy May were quite grown up and had been captured some years before. Daisy was an outstanding cook and prepared the food for the whole dormitory every day. And then there was little Elspeth, the youngest of the lot who would need the most looking after if they were all to get away safely. Tom promised to do his utmost not to leave anyone behind. If one went tonight, they all went.

'How will they get in through the door?' asked Robert Williams. 'It's always locked. Only the Robes have a key.'

Ralph strode quickly over to check the door. It was locked as usual.

For a moment they looked at each other in desperation. How would they reach the boat, if indeed it came at all? They could only hope that their rescuer, whoever it was, had the answer.

Tom gave them all a reassuring smile.

'They must know what they're doing,' he said firmly. 'What we need to do is find a light...'

It was night-time when the boat slid silently across the water towards the landing stage. The lights of the dome cast an eery glow over the surroundings and the dormitory building was just visible in the murky gloom.

To avoid attracting attention, George was in the water, pulling the boat along, while Sam sat by the tiller, steering as best he could. As quietly as possible, they guided the boat towards the landing slip, but couldn't avoid the grinding noise it made as it came to a stop. They all held their breath and listened for some response to the noise, but nothing came. However, in the dormitory windows they could see the curtains twitching as the imprisoned orphans watched them arrive.

Sam leapt out first and ran up to the door. He searched under the stone where George had seen the Robes hide the key. To his delight it was still there. His fingers trembling with excitement, he jammed the key in the lock and turned. The door opened with a rusty creek. Before he could step inside, Milly pushed past him and ran straight into the arms of Tom. For a brief while they hugged and whispered together as George, Sam, Scorpio and

Drago crowded into the dormitory.

The door was closed, the curtains were drawn and the lights were switched on. A lot of handshaking took place as the ten excited prisoners greeted their young rescuers. Sam knew Raffer and Agnes from the orphanage and he smiled as he remembered the twelve-year-old identical twins. They both had button noses, hundreds of freckles and untidy, ginger hair. Sam liked them, in spite of their known fondness for causing mischief whenever possible. He thought back to the time when Raffer sneaked under the table in the dining room and tied the shoelaces of Maude Jones together. Agnes deliberately threw some bread across the table and when Maude Jones stood up to rebuke her, she fell flat on her face. All the children roared with laughter and Raffer sneaked back to his seat unnoticed.

Sam shook their hands and they smiled happily at him. Next to them was their best friend, Charlie Trinder, whom he also recognised, along with several of the other children.

George brought the subdued chatter to a close when he held up his hand.

'We must leave quickly. Please follow Milly and Scorpio into the boat. Each take a blanket with you and stay under cover,' he said.

Robert Williams was the first to make a move and huddled himself up at the front of the boat, where he was soon joined by Charlie Trinder and the twins.

A young girl clutched a bag and smiled shyly

151

at Milly as she passed by her. Tom introduced her as Singer Smith. 'She has a beautiful voice,' he explained. 'The Robes like her to sing for them.'

Then Billy and Daisy May were introduced as they scuttled by, with their blankets draped over their heads. Then came little Elspeth, shivering and stammering with fear. Tom took her hand as he led

her out to the boat.

'It's all right,' he said to her in a calm, reassuring voice. 'I will look after you.'

Ralph brought up the rear, making sure no one was following them.

Once they had all filed out of the door, George remembered some unfinished business. He hissed to Sam, 'Wait for us!' Then, taking Tom by the arm, he led him back into the dormitory and told him about the bag he had seen being given to Barking Mad.

Tom nodded. 'Diamonds,' he said. 'The Robes have lots of them. They're not worth much here, but Barking can't get enough of them.'

George smiled. 'Then I'm sure they won't miss a few.'

Tom was about to object, but George silenced him.

'Look at your friends, look at what's been done to them. Don't they deserve to take something back? Why should Barking get all the reward for their hard work?'

Tom shrugged, then nodded.

'OK,' he said, 'But we must be quick.'

Opening the door leading into the dome, George peered out into the corridor. The lights inside were on and the machinery still hummed and gave off its heat. He led the way up the stairs and, after a quick glance into the room to make sure it was empty, they opened the door and slipped inside.

'They're in this drawer,' whispered George, and he went round the table and pulled it. But it wouldn't open.

'Locked!' he said, looking round for something he could use to prise the drawer open.

'Hardly surprising, is it?' said a deep voice. Both of them froze.

The light was turned on in the room and, jerking up their heads, they saw Jethro Barking filling the doorway with his bulky frame.

'Well, well, well!' he roared. 'My little escapees! I was wondering where you'd got to!' Stepping back into the corridor, he turned his head and roared again. This time it was for help. 'Alarm! We have intruders!'

George and Tom looked for a way out, but Barking Mad's huge bulk blocked the door entirely. Then, eager to get his hands on the two of them, he stepped forwards with arms outstretched.

'Got you now, you can't escape!' he screamed, his puffy face turning red. 'I'll teach you a lesson you won't forget!'

As he came closer, Tom lifted one end of the table and shoved it at the headmaster, hitting him square in the stomach and making him stumble. Seeing their chance, George and Tom darted round the table and headed towards the door. With Barking Mad struggling on the floor as they passed, George stopped and looked down. There, bulging in Barking's waistcoat pocket, he saw the leather bag of diamonds.

'Come on, George!' shouted Tom from the door. 'We have to go!'

Reaching down, George tore open the pocket and grabbed the small bundle. Yanking it out, he heard Barking Mad screaming after him as he joined Tom in the corridor.

'Got it!' he shouted proudly, and together the two of them raced towards the stairs, Barking's cries echoing after them.

As they ran, Robes appeared from rooms all along the corridor, peering out to see what the fuss was. But before they could even register the intruders, Tom and George had already darted past and got to the staircase. Behind them, Jethro Barking, back on his feet, was in hot pursuit, roaring like a crazed lion.

At the foot of the stairs they skidded across the floor into the dormitory, which was now empty, and slammed the door behind them.

'Quick,' cried George. 'Help me!' He grabbed the nearest bed. Tom understood, and the two of them dragged the bed across the floor and jammed it up against the closed door.

'That should hold them for a few minutes,' said Tom, as they ran along the dormitory towards the door at the far end.

'Go, go, go!' shouted George as he appeared in the doorway and saw Sam waiting by the boat. As he and Tom ran out, Tom slammed the door, locked it and flung the key way out into the moat. It landed with a distant plop!

As Sam pushed the boat into the water, George ran up and in one great stride leapt into the middle of it, falling in a heap amongst the other passengers. Tom was right behind him and dived over Sam, landing in another heap right on top of George. Sam scrambled after him and pulled the cord to start the engine. It spluttered, and died.

'Pull harder!' shouted George.

Angry fists were banging now at the locked

dormitory door.

Taking a deep breath, Sam gave it all he had and pulled the cord again. The engine sprang to life and, grabbing the tiller, he began to turn the boat out towards the middle of the moat. But the boat was heavy, and its movement slow.

The locked door burst open now and Jethro Barking, followed by several other Robes, ran out into the night screaming and hollering. Without stopping, he ran down the slipway, still roaring with anger, and straight into the water. With a desperate dive, he managed to grab the back of the boat with both hands.

With his great quivering bulk hanging on to it, the boat moved out into the deeper waters of the moat. Giving out another roar, the angry, purple-faced headmaster heaved himself out of the water and began to clamber into the boat. The other children screamed and began to clamber in a panic towards the prow in an effort to get away from him. But one child stood firm, no longer afraid of this roaring brute before her.

As Jethro Barking hooked his leg over the side of the boat and began to clamber inside, Milly stepped up to him and looked him straight in the eye.

'Where do you think you're going?' she asked, in a voice so firm and direct, that it took him quite by surprise.

'Huh?' was all he could think of to say and, before anything else occurred to him, Milly gave him a shove so hard, that he actually flew a few feet backwards before landing in the water with a great splash.

As the boat, relieved of his extra weight, began to move more quickly through the water, the occupants heard the sound of a lot of thrashing and splashing about, with a few muffled gurgled cries. Then Sam saw something moving in the water.

'Look!' he cried. 'What's that?'

It was dark, and the glow of the lamps on the Dome offered little by way of illumination, but George, looking out, knew exactly what it was Sam had seen.

'It's the shark!' he said.

As they watched in stunned silence, the black fin moved rapidly in a straight line right for the flailing, struggling bulk of Jethro Barking.

A sudden shriek from Jethro told the children he had seen the shark too. Now they watched as he turned his attention towards reaching the bank as fast as he could. There was some splashing and scuffling, but as they drifted further away, darkness fell on the scene and none of them could really see what was going on. A loud roar split the night. Was it in anger? In pain? None of them could tell. One thing, however, they knew for sure.

'That sounds like Jethro,' said Tom.

'It does indeed,' answered George.

George took control of the boat and, for the rest of the night, steered it at full speed out of the moat and back into the river that led to the Rainbow Cave. Although it was still dark, a clear sky promised another warm day ahead. But for now it was cold and the children sat, bunched together, huddled up in their blankets.

Milly was lying in the back of the boat with Tom on one side and Sam on the other. The three of them looked up at the sky as the boat chugged on through the still waters.

'Why is the weather here so different from back home?' asked Sam at last. The question had been bothering him for some time now.

'Climate control,' said Tom. 'That's what they call it. It's something to do with the big doughnut thing in the engine room.'

Robert Williams, the budding scientist of the group, chipped in.

'I believe that there is a massive power source of some sort deep in the ground that produces unlimited energy. The engines above, and the doughnut, as you call it, are all part of the system for harnessing this energy. Though the Robes have built the engines, they are frightened of the energy source, so they bring us in to do the work needed to keep all the energy within controlled parameters.'

'Who are the Robes, and these Minlings? Where did they come from?'

'I don't know for sure, but I think they are the descendants of a people who arrived here many thousands of years ago, if not more.'

'Arrived from where?' asked Sam, now feeling

totally confused. 'Do you mean they've come from abroad?'

'Further than that,' said Robert, and pulled his blanket tight around him. 'It's all very strange and magical, but for now all I want to do is get back to the real world and away from these Robes for good.'

'Me too,' added Tom. 'They're a nasty bunch, and up to no good, I bet!'

'Do you know what happens in the Rainbow Cave that causes all the changes?' asked Milly.

'No,' said Robert. 'I have no idea. They covered us up when we came through it, so I didn't see a thing.'

Drago chipped in. 'You'd best be covered up when we go back through as well, all of you. There's no telling what might happen otherwise.'

'I'd rather like to be changed,' said Charlie Trinder, looking at Milly with admiration. 'I'd like to be as strong as her. Did you see her push old Barking? He fairly flew through the air!'

Tom smiled. 'She's always been a tough one,' he said, with a glance at his sister.

'I've heard the Robes say that the changes can be bad as well as good.' said Ralph, visibly nervous at the thought of going through the cave again. 'You could lose your sight, or your memory, or the use of your legs... Perhaps Milly was just lucky.'

'Well,' said Tom. 'If she was, then we're lucky she's on our side!'

A cheer of agreement went up, then all the

children settled down and grew silent, preparing themselves for the long journey home.

Through a faint early morning light George could see both banks of the main river now and, with a feeling of relief, he settled down for the long ride to the Rainbow Cave, his hand firmly on the tiller, keeping a steady course.

The engine throbbed quietly away and, despite frequent checks, there appeared to be no pursuit from behind. Some of the children had fallen asleep, but most were too excited, or nervous, to settle down and kept staring over the side in case of danger.

'Watch out for crocodiles,' advised George, ever mindful of their earlier encounter with the beasts.

It was a simple whistle from behind that alerted them to danger. All eyes turned to look back, straining to see what had caused the whistle, but there was nothing to be seen. A few minutes later another series of whistles made them sit upright and stare back again. This time lights could be seen strung out across the river and getting steadily closer. The Robes were in hot pursuit.

Although George had the engine full on, the extra load of all the children slowed them down and meant that the boats behind were travelling a little bit faster.

'Everyone get to the back,' he cried. With the prow raised slightly, George hoped he might get a little more speed out of the boat.

As the children began to move back, Billy May called out in alarm and pointed up river.

'Look! What's that?'

They all swivelled round to look. Up ahead, glowing green lights were floating in the air and approaching them. Crouching down in the boat the children watched with apprehension.

'Night vultures!' called out Scorpio, and promptly dived into the cabin.

'Night vultures?' cried Sam. 'What are night vultures?'

'Bad news, I think,' said Drago, and followed Scorpio down into the cabin.

Moments later, a large bird hovered over them, its wings flapping slowly up and down. A green glow emanated from the feathers on its body like an eerie torch, lighting up the night air around it. A long neck, supporting a small, bald head, bent down and glowing eyes stared at them. Its savage beak was curved to a sharp point, and its claws were splayed out at the end of short, stubby legs.

Soon the whole boat was illuminated by a green glow as more of the birds hovered all round them. The children all crammed themselves into the cabin behind Scorpio and Drago. Only George, Sam, Milly and Tom stayed outside and watched with growing fear as the birds started to cackle and crow. With a scratchy bump, one of them landed on the front of the boat and started to hop along the roof of the cabin towards them.

Scorpio appeared in the doorway of the cabin. 'They're killers!' he shouted. 'Very nasty. Hide!'

Three of the birds landed on the boat. One was heading towards Milly, it's sharp beak open, hissing and spitting. She raised her fists, and the bird raised its claws. With a vicious cackle and a great flap of its wings, it was just about to bear down on her when a grey, hairy blur shot out of the cabin with a growling roar.

Before the bird could react, Drago planted himself firmly in front of Milly. Slowly he advanced on the cackling bird, whose cackling turned to a screech when it saw the anger in Drago's eyes. Losing its balance, the bird toppled over the side of the boat, then had to flap madly to get back into the air before it crashed into the water.

The remaining vultures now backed off and flapped their way back into the air to rejoin their companions, who were apparently beginning to think twice about attacking this particular boat. The retreating vultures set up a cacophony of sound as they retreated, eventually settling in the branches of a lifeless tree on the riverbank.

'Well done, Drago,' said Sam. 'Perfect timing!'

Tom stared at the dog, shrinking slowly back to his normal size.

'That's a useful pet,' he said at last.

'Don't call me a pet,' muttered Drago, as he jumped off the roof of the boat and settled down in the hold once again. 'It really doesn't suit me.'

Whilst Drago settled, George took the tiller and set about getting the boat back on course. Aware that the flotilla was still behind them, he hoped they might just have enough time to reach the Rainbow Cave before being captured. If they could get inside, then they could hide in the mist like they had before, and hopefully make it through in one piece.

As to what would happen then, he had no idea...

BACK IN LITTLEWICH

When dawn arrived, the flotilla was still on their tail. The shouts they heard from the pursuing craft indicated that the Robes could see them. There were about a dozen boats similar to their own, stretched out across the river, forming a barrage to prevent their doubling back.

'We'll be safe if we can reach the cave,' said George anxiously. 'Once we're in that lake, the mist and the strange lights will make us hard to find.'

He spoke more in hope than from any absolute certainty.

Looking ahead, he saw the cliffs and the entrance to the cave were not much further away. Milly jumped up beside him.

'We're going to make it,' she cried, her voice brimming with excitement.

'Not if you don't keep still,' growled George, pulling the tiller sharply to keep the boat on course. He found the action heavy and the motor began to grind with a low, moaning sound.

'We're slowing down,' called Tom. 'What's happening?'

Sam looked over the side of the boat, to be confronted by a vision of green, gooey slime floating on the water. 'Weeds!' he shouted 'Thick weeds everywhere.'

The boat came to a shuddering halt. The weed surrounded it on all sides. Excited shouts came from the Robes as they saw their quarry become entangled and stuck. Looking over the side, his heart pounding in desperation, George saw finger-like fronds reaching out from the weed and waving about. Each frond had little suckers down one side. Whenever one of these suckers touched the side of the boat, it stuck tightly to the wood. Other suckers followed suit and so, bit by bit, the fronds climbed their way up the sides of the boat.

Trying to pull them off was useless. By the time one or two suckers had been removed, two or three more had already fastened themselves on.

'If this goes on, we'll be pulled under,' cried Sam.

'Pass me the end of that rope,' ordered George, pointing to a coiled up bundle in the centre of the boat. One of the twins snatched it up and gave it to him. 'Fasten the other end to the front of the boat,' he said and stood up.

'What are you going to do?' asked Milly.

'The weed floats on the surface, so I'm going under the water and I'll drag the boat through to the cave. Keep pulling those suckers off. Once we start moving, they won't be able to grab us so easily. Hurry now, we haven't much time.'

Wrapping the rope around his waist George dived into the lake. He went right through the weed and, to his relief, found clear water underneath.

Swimming back to the stern, he found that the weed had wrapped itself around the propeller and jammed it fast. With a great deal of heaving and pulling, he managed to free the blades. Suddenly, the engine sprang to life and was able to move the propeller again. Turning away, he swam powerfully in the direction of the cave, clutching the rope tight around his chest.

Up above, the children, who had all been desperately pulling at the fronds, gave a cheer when the boat started to move forwards again. Slowly at first, they began to break free from the blanket of weed. As it proceeded to clear, the boat moved much more quickly. Under the water, George was straining his muscles against the weight, pulling the

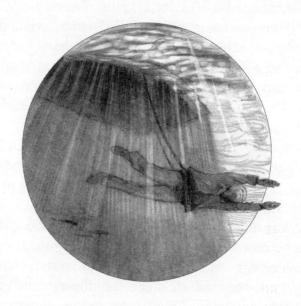

boat along with all his might.

Seeing them moving off, the pursuing flotilla inched forward, but soon they too were caught by the sucking weed. Feeling themselves to be breaking free, and seeing their pursuers getting entangled, the children on the boat dared to let out a mighty cheer.

Surely now they were safe...

The tunnel entrance that loomed up in front of them was dark and forbidding. Free of the weed, George climbed back on board and took control of the tiller again. Slowly they slipped into the dark, cold passage, bumping along the walls as they had before, until an eery light ahead indicated that the lake was not far off.

'Everyone get inside,' called George. 'And cover yourselves with blankets!'

All the children, along with Drago and Scorpio, crowded down below as fast as they could. Only George, Sam and Milly remained above decks.

'You too,' cried George. 'Cover yourselves!'

Quickly, the three of them pulled the blankets over their heads and crouched down as much as they could.

A short while later they became aware of the familiar humming noise of the cave. The light slowly changed to a bright pink that grew steadily stronger until the lake and the boat were bathed in a fulsome red. As they moved on through the water, the light gradually passed from red to orange, then yellow and so on through all the colours of the rainbow.

Finally, just as the last violet light faded, Sam spotted the way out. He was sitting at the very front of the boat and staring intently into the swirling mist. 'There it is! A tunnel right ahead of us,' he called out.

George adjusted the tiller slightly and steered the boat towards the black hole that led to the exit from the Rainbow Cave. Once inside the tunnel, George gave the all clear and the fugitive passengers, one by one, crawled out of the cabin and sat around the edges of the boat as it bumped and lurched its way along the dank, gloomy passage.

Sam clambered to the back of the boat. 'Do you think we can escape through Littlewich?' he asked George as he sat down next to him.

George thought for a moment, then shrugged.

'I'm not sure. If the Robes have sent word through, then it will be difficult. At least this time there are more of us, and we have powers we never dreamed about before.'

He smiled at Sam, who smiled back. They both knew it was hopeful talk, but it was better by far to be hopeful than to despair.

George carried on, in a quieter voice so that the others would not hear. 'I think our big problem is getting back through the hedge. We have to find someone who knows the secret of how to make it open up.'

'I know that,' said Tom, who was sitting nearby

and listening in. George and Sam stared at him.

'It's true,' he explained. 'When I was taken and carried through the hedge I remember hearing a voice, really irritable and demanding. I realise now it was one of the Robes, but I heard him say, "Twist the square branch, you nincompoop!" He was telling someone how to close the hedge.'

George thought for a moment. 'How to close it,' he said at last. 'But what about opening it?'

'It must be the same, surely!' said Sam hopefully.

George shrugged.

'Trouble is,' added Tom, looking suddenly quite crestfallen. 'I don't know where the square branch is, and the hedge goes on for miles...' He slumped back down with a heavy sigh.

'We know!' chipped in Milly, who had also been listening to the conversation. 'George tied a handkerchief at the spot where the hedge closed, so the square branch must be there somewhere.'

This brightened Tom up, but George still looked bothered.

'Let's hope it's still there,' he said. 'Anything could have happened to it...'

A soft voice called from the prow.

'I see a light ahead!' Singer Smith was now acting as lookout at the front of the boat. 'We're coming out of the cave.'

George slowed the boat down and allowed the river to float them gently into the daylight.

A small black form dropped down in front of them, its wings flapping in a frantic manner.

'Watch out, watch out! They're everywhere!'

The familiar shrill voice of Batty echoed round the tunnel. She was wheeling and turning in the air above their heads. Her excited voice alerted them and, sitting bolt upright, everyone stared into the brightness ahead.

'Faster, go faster!' shrieked Batty. 'Too slow, too slow.'

Handing the tiller to Tom, George sprang to the front of the boat just as it cleared the tunnel. There were a few moments of blinking while his eyes adjusted to the bright light, but then he saw what he had feared most - a great circle of boats lined up ahead of them. His heart leapt into his throat.

'Oh no...' he groaned in a low, defeated voice. But then, as his eyesight became clearer, he spotted a gap between two of the smaller boats, just big enough for the barge to get through, if it pushed hard enough. Grabbing the rope again, he dived straight into the water.

Tom turned up the engine to maximum speed and, with George pulling it, the barge headed right for the gap. In the waiting craft, many orange gowns indicated a heavy presence of Robes among the massed throngs of Minlings. They too had seen the weakness in their line and, with a great deal of shouting and waving, directed the boats to move closer together and close the gap to prevent any escape. But the loud cries sent up by the Robes and their cohorts were suddenly cut short as George, hidden from view under the surface, took up the challenge and swam as hard as he could for the narrowing gap.

With his power, coupled with the engine at full burst, there was no way the barge was going to stop. George was pulling as hard as he had ever pulled before and the boat skimmed along the surface, as though about to take off and fly. The gap had almost closed as they neared it, and a Robe in one of the smaller boats on the starboard side reached out to grab the side of their boat in an attempt to climb on board. His hood had fallen back to reveal a craggy face with small, sharp eyes that gleamed at the anticipated capture.

But the Robe had made a mistake in his calculations...

The boat was going too fast for him and, before he even saw it coming, Milly's arm swept him away like a dry leaf. The commotion of the Robe crashing backwards caused his boat to rock furiously and bump into the one alongside it. This set up a bobbing motion, made worse by the wake of the barge as it sped past. One by one, Minlings and Robes began to lose their footing and topple over. Some fell onto the decks whilst others were flung even further and fell overboard.

The resulting chaos caused pandemonium amongst the ranks of would-be captors, and many desperate cries went up from those swept into the water. Neither Robes, nor Minlings, had a great fondness for getting wet.

On the other side of the speeding barge, Raffer,

held tightly by his sister, had leaned out with an oar in both hands, and swiped it skillfully at the Robes lined up ready to jump at them. The swinging oar knocked them down like skittles, setting a similar commotion on the port side, as the boat burst through the gap and into open water.

George swam on for as far as he could go, but then he too had to rest. Exhausted, he climbed back into the barge and fell in a heap on the floor, gasping to get the air back into his lungs.

Behind them, the chaotic armada were attempting to turn and give chase, but so many of their number were now floating in the water, flapping their arms and crying out for help, that those left in the boats had no idea where to turn first. Seizing their chance, Sam cranked up the engine once more and set the barge on course to get as far away as possible as quickly as possible.

After a short while, they saw the warehouse quay looming up ahead, and Jangle, standing on his chair by the door and clapping his hands in delight. Above them, Batty was cackling and screeching. Throughout their dash to escape, the excited bird had been dive bombing and shouting at the Robes in an effort to slow them down. Now she was celebrating their escape and finally she zoomed down to alight on the prow of the boat, flapping her wings in great excitement.

'Brilliant!' she shouted. 'I enjoyed that. You showed the monsters how to fight.' She gave out a long, cackling laugh. 'Did you see them all falling in the water...'

Jangle laughed too, then added, in a more cautious tone, 'Now what? You have to keep going. Where will you head?'

'To the hedge, as fast as we can,' said George.

'In which case, you had better stop before you reach the bridge.'

Up ahead, they saw the bridge where they had rescued Batty. The shortest way across the fields to the hedge was under the bridge and on a bit further.

'Why?' asked George. 'There's nobody on the bridge, and no boats in our way.'

Jangle shook his head and looked very serious.

'They're hiding on the bridge, and they have a great pile of stones and rocks all stored up to drop on you as you go under.'

'The beasts!' snarled Milly.

'In that case,' said George, 'we have to stop here and make a run for it towards the hill. The Muttons only come out at night, so we should be quite safe.'

'They mostly come out at night,' Drago cut in, and added in a worried voice, 'but they have been known to come out in the day if they get woken up.'

'Woken up by what?' asked Sam.

'Vibrations. They hear them in their hollows you see.'

'Vibrations of what?'

'Running feet,' said Drago sternly. 'We have sixteen pairs of them between us. That's bound to reach their ears.'

There was a horrified silence. The boat bumped

softly against the quay.

'We just have to run very, very quickly then,' George said quietly. 'We have the element of surprise, and the Muttons move slowly. By the time they are aware that we are on the green, we'll be past them and on our way to the hedge.'

He looked around at all the worried faces.

'It's our only chance!'

One by one, they all gave a nervous smile and nodded. Grabbing the tiller, Sam engaged the engine and started to turn the boat towards the far bank of the river.

'Goodbye,' called Jangle as they drifted away. 'And good luck!'

'You can do it. I know you can!' cried Batty, and flew up into the air to watch their progress.

Hitting the muddy bank with a great force, the barge slithered up onto the damp grass and came to a halt. All the occupants leapt out in an orderly fashion and gathered at the top of the rise.

'Now then, you all heard what Drago said,' said George. 'We need to run as quietly as we can, but as fast as we can. Got that?'

Ten faces nodded and Scorpio scratched his head. Drago shook his and licked a front paw.

Together they started moving in the direction of the hedge, the top of which could just be seen in the distance. As they did so, a crowd of Minlings and Robes came running at them from every direction.

As one, the escapees started to sprint, leaving all thoughts of stealth behind. Singer Smith was by far the slowest of the group and, with his new found power, Sam was very much the fastest. Even little Elspeth could get up quite a surprising speed when she had to.

As the pursuing hoard closed in, thirteen children, one Minling and a dog raced for their lives across the vast expanse of green that lay between them and the hedge. Behind the hedge was safety, but before they could be sure of that, they would all have to reach the hedge and, somehow, get through it.

At first the Robes, who were bigger and quicker than the Minlings, gained rapidly on the party, and especially on Singer Smith who had managed to lose her shoes and was now lagging far behind the others.

Drawing up sharply, Sam turned back to help Singer, with Drago in support. In one scoop, Sam picked her up in his arms and set off at top speed to catch up with the others. As he went, Drago stood his ground to face the oncoming pursuers. A few snarls and barks, plus the sight of him slowly growing in size, caused them to hesitate and hold back. In that moment, Drago turned too and ran to join his friends.

When Sam had what he felt to be a large enough lead, he put Singer Smith down and raced back to help anyone else who couldn't keep up. Tom and Robert Williams were keeping up with George. Behind them the twins led the rest in a scattered bunch who ran with legs pumping hard and heads thrown back in the terrifying dash to safety. Suffering most was Scorpio, who struggled to move very quickly at all. On either side of him, Billy and Daisy May had stopped to help and now half pulled, half carried him.

As Sam arrived to help, he noticed that the pursuers had stopped chasing them. Instead, they stood as one great crowd, all gathered together in a large huddle.

With growing relief, he called out to the others, 'Stop, slow down! They've given up, we're safe!'

One by one the children slowed to an exhausted halt and, hands on knees, catching their breath, looked behind them. To their amazement, the crowd of people had begun to jump on the spot. They could be seen bobbing up and down together and shouting in rhythmic voices. The ground seemed to throb with the noise.

'Oh no,' groaned Drago, with a low growl. 'They're calling up the Muttons.'

'Come on!' shouted George from the front. 'Keep going!' Even as he spoke, the ground in front of him buckled and bulged and a small lump appeared. The lump got bigger very quickly, then split apart to reveal the head of a Mutton, eyes glowing, mouth snarling and its red teeth slavering.

For a moment, George stood rooted to the ground, staring at the fearsome creature before him. He watched in horrified fascination as the Mutton heaved itself out of the ground and slowly shook itself to clear the soil off its woolly coat.

George took a step back, but then another lump appeared beside him, and another just beyond that. Looking round he saw that all over the green, Muttons were emerging from the ground and shaking themselves.

A piercing scream rang out behind him. Spinning round, he saw Singer Smith rooted to the ground with three Muttons advancing slowly towards her.

'Run!' shouted George. 'Any way you can!'

He tried to reach her, but Sam had seen the danger too and raced past George at a remarkable speed. Just as the Muttons were set to attack the terrified girl, he again scooped her up and whisked her away from their vicious jaws. Instead of falling on their prey, the three Muttons fell on each other, already excited by the smell of fear.

The group started running again, more slowly this time, swerving in and out of the emerging Muttons. At first it was easy, but as they neared the hedge, it became more difficult as Muttons appeared thick and fast. Soon it would be impossible to avoid them.

George called out to Sam who, although he carried Singer Smith, was still able to run faster than any of them.

'Go ahead,' he shouted. 'Find the square branch!'

Sam turned and raced ahead.

One by one the group finally reached the hedge which loomed up high over them, a wall of knotted, twisted spikes. They started to run again, keeping close to the tangled branches, following Sam who could be seen up ahead checking the branches for the white handkerchief.

He had stopped running and, fixed as he was on finding the right branch, failed to notice the Muttons converging on him from behind. It would only be a matter of time before the Muttons surrounded him.

As the rest of the children got close, Sam cried out in delight.

'Got it!'

He had found the white handkerchief and now started looking for the square branch.

'Sam!' cried Milly. 'Watch out!'

The Muttons approached relentlessly.

The branch proved elusive. All of them were searching for it now, wriggling into the hedge as far as they could go, despite the thorns, or jumping up to see if it was up above their heads.

'It's here somewhere,' screeched Milly in a panic, as the Muttons joined together in a great semicircle and moved a few more paces towards them. Drago turned to face them, snarling, growling and growing in size for all he was worth. They were surrounded now. There was no escape. Their lives depended on finding the square branch.

'It could be further up,' shouted George, stepping back and looking keenly into the high branches of the hedge.

Raffer lifted Agnes onto his shoulders and the girl suddenly pointed upwards. 'I see it! It's a big branch, right above me. Keep still Raffer, I have to jump.'

Agnes steadied herself by holding onto the hedge with one hand and standing on her brother's shoulders. Staring at the square branch above her, she bent her knees and sprang into the air with her arms outstretched.

It was a desperate dive, but she made it.

Both hands wrapped around the branch and grasped it tightly; her weight began to lower the branch and soon Tom and Ralph could reach it as well. George joined them and together they heaved it right down to the ground.

The hedge opened. Slowly at first, the small branches started to straighten, then suddenly there was a loud noise like the crackling of a million breaking twigs. All the tangled branches within the dense hedge straightened into thousands of slim, vertical poles that reached up high into the sky. As soon as it was possible, the children wriggled past the upright branches and squeezed through to the other side.

Raffer and Tom were the last children through, and Drago the last of all. Just behind them, the Muttons stopped short of the hedge. A solid flock of them stood shoulder to shoulder, nose to tail, and simply watched their prey escape. For a few moments the group of children looked back through the gap in the hedge where the line of Muttons stood. There was silence on both sides. A shocked, exhausted silence from the children, and a resigned, indifferent silence from the Muttons.

Then the hedge started to close. Again, it crackled and snapped, and soon the hedge had reverted to its normal state and all was silent in the air.

Singer and Daisy May cried with relief, the twins cheered and the rest of them soon joined in. With their arms around each other, the group slowly trudged along the path in the direction of the orphanage. There was really nowhere else to go and, since they knew that Old Barking Mad would not be there to greet them, they were no longer frightened of Maude Jones, or anyone else.

After a moment George broke off from the group. He picked up a heavy rock from the side of the path and carried it back to the spot where the hedge had closed. Sam watched him and waited until George caught up with him again.

'You never know,' said George with a smile. 'I never, ever want to go back there, but you never know.'

Sam slapped him on the back. 'Come on,' he said. 'Let's go and see what's going on indoors.'

EPILOGUE

It was dark when the bedraggled travellers reached the Mercy Hall Home for Orphans. The first thing they noticed was a square sign hanging from a pole which read, 'FOR SALE'. A few candles flickered in the windows of the ground floor and an oil lamp could be seen illuminating the kitchen window at the side of the big house. Otherwise all was quiet.

George led the children and Drago to the kitchen door and opened it.

Mrs Gertrude Armitage was a small, rotund woman somewhere around her middle age. She had been the cook at the home for about a year. Not one for unexpected surprises, she generally took to them very badly. When the door opened quite suddenly and the children crowded into the kitchen looking tired, bedraggled and starving, she took one look at them, and screamed.

It was George who finally calmed her down.

'What are you lot doing here?' she asked in a breathless, agitated voice. 'You're not supposed to be here. Go away, all of you.' She frowned as she spoke and looked angry. After a glance down at the table, she mumbled something to herself, then looked at them again and continued.

'There's nothing for you here, nothing at all! I'm closing the house down and leaving tonight.'

George followed her glance at the table, and saw it was covered in food. A slab of ham in its muslin cloth, a sack of potatoes, three chickens ready for plucking and several loaves of bread were stacked next to a sack of flour.

'And taking all the food with you as well,' added Sam, who had also noticed the potential feast lying before them.

Mrs Armitage bristled with indignation. 'And why not? There are no children left here anymore, and I have a new position in London. I'm off as soon as the coach arrives.'

'Why are you closing down? Where are the children?' asked Milly.

'Jiggery pokery,' snorted Mrs Armitage. 'Old Barking's disappeared, and the Jones woman has done a runner. The house is to be sold by the bank to pay off all the debts.'

George frowned.

'I knew about Barking,' he said, in a general sort of way. 'But Jones?'

'Don't ask me,' said Mrs Armitage, bustling around the room with bags full of groceries. 'I'm only glad to be going myself. If you want more information, better ask the bank!'

'Well,' said George, stepping out of her way. 'We are still here, and we are all staying until alternative arrangements can be made.' He was glad Maude Jones was also gone, but alarmed at the thought that there would soon be nowhere for them to live.

The sound of horse's hooves grating on the path heralded a coach drawing up outside the door. Mrs Armitage became very agitated indeed. 'Oh, deary me,' she kept muttering to herself. 'This ain't right at all...'

Presently, a burly man in a dark green greatcoat appeared in the doorway.

'What's all this 'ere?' he growled, scowling at the children. 'I thought all these blighters had gone. Come on Gertrude, grab the stuff and let's be on our way.'

He shoved his way through the children, picked up a heavy box from the table, and turned to leave.

With his foot, he pushed Singer Smith out of the way and the poor, frail girl gave a meek, tired whimper.

Before he could take another step forward, Milly confronted him.

'Please put the box down,' she said very politely. 'We still live here and will be needing food and provisions for the next few days, so please put it back.'

The man sneered and, ignoring her completely, made to push past her and head for the door. But he stopped in his tracks when Drago emerged from the gathered throng and stood firmly in his path. For a moment, the burly man looked undecided. Then Drago growled, the hairs the dog's back stood on end and he moved forwards.

'Push off you lot!' the man said, staring at the dog. 'We are taking everything we can carry, and that's that. This place is finished!'

Drago growled again, and the man jumped back a step. Then, seeming to have a sudden, inexplicable change of mind, he placed the box carefully back on the table and edged his way over towards Gertrude Armitage.

George approached the cook, an idea forming in his mind.

'You had better go, both of you. In spite of the imminent change in ownership, we will be staying here for the foreseeable future, and you can be sure we won't let you remove anything from the house.'

To emphasise the point he stepped to one side and waved them to the door. The rest of the children automatically moved out of the way and a narrow pathway opened up. Sam also gestured towards the door with his arm and the rest of the children followed suit. The cook and the burly man had no other option than to leave empty handed, which they did, scowling and glaring as they went. As one, the children followed them outside and watched as the coach, pulled by two raggedy grey horses, drove off down the drive.

Returning to the kitchen door, they were surprised by a small dog, a wirehaired terrier with patches of black over its head and shoulders, which came running round the corner barking in a most excited manner.

'Scruffy!' yelled Milly, as the lost pet jumped straight into her arms. 'Where have you been?' she said, as she hugged him. In answer the little dog yapped and licked at her cheeks.

Daisy May, Singer and Agnes immediately set to and prepared bread, cheese and cold meats for everyone while the boys searched around the building for any other stragglers. Once they were sure they had the place to themselves, they gathered in the familiar dining room and sat round the table to eat.

'I have an idea,' said George standing up on a bench to address the assembled company. 'We are all orphans of various ages. Some of us are more grown up than others, but we all have one thing in common - none of us has anywhere to live. I believe we should stick together, buy this house and live here.'

There was a stunned silence as they all thought about this strange and wonderful idea.

Raffer frowned and scratched his head

'Great idea, but how can we possibly buy this place?'

George smiled. 'Diamonds,' he said, and reached into his pocket. Pulling out the small leather bag, he emptied the contents onto the table for all to see.

There were gasps all round as the diamonds tumbled out and landed in a sparkling crescent on the table. Everyone reached out to touch and study the precious stones. None of them had ever seen diamonds before, and it was hard to believe that these shiny bits of hard crystal were valuable enough to buy them a whole orphanage...

By the door, a large dog settled itself down for a rest and said, 'Well, I wonder what tomorrow will bring.'

Beside him, a small dog sat eagerly wagging its tail, but said nothing.

Outside the room, a little fellow, with a hunched back and dark, floppy hair, found a broom and began to sweep...

COMING SOON...

The Thorn Gate Trilogy
Book Two

LITTLEWICH   NOGOODLANDS

MARKET TOWNE

SECRETS OF
MERCY
HALL

Written by **Garth Edwards**   Illustrated by **Max Stasyuk**